ROSIE & THE SHADOW PEOPLE

By A.M. Sandoval

To Velma, my beloved pup.

CHAPTER 1

I'm sitting in the backseat of my dad's car and I don't know where we are. There are endless flat green fields between Illinois and California that roll into mountains and grow yellower as we make our way west.

I spend much of the drive in a kind of suspended animation. I try to read my "Fear Street" book, but I get carsick. I sketch the red rock formations that reach out like claws toward the sky in Utah, but the ride is too bumpy and the sketches look like chicken scratch. Mostly, I just sit and stare out the window. Everything blurs as we whiz past the blaring lights of Las Vegas and finally cross over the state line into the darkness of the Mojave Desert. It's here that I finally break the hours of silence.

"Dad, aren't there earthquakes in California?" I ask.

"Sure there are," he says, elevating his voice slightly. Dad has a way of sounding excited by nearly anything, even something terrible like an earthquake, and convincing you that should be excited, too. "But it's just like we have tornados sometimes back home. You just … duck down and hold on. It's nothing to worry about, Rosie."

"Rosie." I mouth it to myself in the window reflection, watching my lips curl around the "O." I have no idea how that name's going to sound to other kids in my new school. I wonder how it will look written down.

Aubrey Rose O'Connell is my name, but my dad has sometimes called me Rosie when he's trying to be funny, like the way that he calls himself Danny instead of Dan or Daniel. Lately he does it more and more, finally suggesting using it as my first name as a way to leave the past behind. Something he read in a psychiatry book about dealing with loss, I guess. I finally decide I kind of like it. I'm done with Aubrey. She sounds like a sad, brown-haired girl that reads all the time—which I am. But I'm going to be someone different in the seventh grade. "Rosie" sounds more exciting.

I write the name in cursive in the moisture left by my breath on the window. It looks weird and unfamiliar to me, but I think I can get used to it. I see my faint reflection in the window as the patch of moisture dissipates, and it looks distorted, like some sort of monster that almost looks like me. *God, I wish I was prettier*, I think, staring at the sloping nose I inherited from my Dad's side of the family. *I'd have such an easier time at this new school if I was a little taller and didn't still have this baby fat on my cheeks. I guess I'm still not done going through those good ol' "changes" I've heard so much about — from school (so awkward) and from Dad (horrible). I don't even recognize myself right now.*

"What does Karen think of California?" Dad asks, interrupting my train of thought (which was headed over the cliff into low self-esteem anyway).

Ugh. I don't say anything and neither does Karen, obviously. She's a troll doll that I've had since I was six. And not one of those new troll dolls you get at KB Toys; Karen's an original.

My mind drifts to the real Karen — I named the doll after my next-door neighbor when I was growing up in Galena. Karen was a rough-and-tumble girl with short brown hair, ADD and five cats, varying from kitten to grandma cat. Karen and I would play in the dirt, digging up rolly pollies and building elaborate dirt castles to put them in. Seriously, one time we made a whole rolly polly royal family. Yeah, we were weird.

We'd ride bikes side by side and swing on the swing set, trying to get as high up as possible without breaking our synchronization. We were like twins separated at birth.

But at some point, things changed. Karen wasn't allowed to come over anymore; I didn't know why. I would find one of her cats wandering around our yard and bring it to Karen's front door as an excuse to see her. Her mom would just take the cat, tight-lipped, then she'd thank me and close the door. Three of Karen's cats died over the course of a couple of years, run over by cars speeding down the highway that ran just in front of the houses in our tourist-trap town. I thought, one day, her mom would finally let us play together again and I could tell her how sorry I was about her poor cats. But I never got the chance. Her family moved away before long.

I was devastated when they left. Mom gave me the troll doll as a gift to cheer me up. "She was mine when I was a girl, about your age," she told me. "I never had a name for her, though. Why don't you name her after Karen?"

Even though I missed real Karen a lot, I loved the doll. I'd pretend the real Karen was still there and talk to the doll as if it were actually her, coming up with elaborate playtime scenarios — we were sisters that could communicate telepathically with her cats' spirits to solve neighborhood trouble — allowing me to play quietly, entirely in my own mind. I preferred it that way; anyway, I didn't have many other friends.

I think Mom pretty soon regretted her decision to give me the doll. "She spends all day and all night with that doll," I overheard her saying one day, as I was standing in my Care Bears pajamas with my ear pressed to the bedroom door. "Sometimes she talks to it. She even talks to that poor girl's dead cats. Honestly, Dan, it's not normal."

"It's fine," my dad told her. "Didn't you talk to that thing too as a girl? She's got a great imagination, like her dad. Just leave her to it."

3

I never wanted to worry Mom, but there wasn't much I could do about that. She was really religious and seemingly afraid of her own shadow. Talking to dead cats was off the menu of normal behavior.

But Mom came around — after all, she was the one who gave me the doll and suggested I name it after my only childhood friend. She even sometimes asked about Karen the doll as if she were real, in a way that disturbed the little world I'd created for us. I wondered if that was on purpose.

I think she just knew I wasn't quite normal and tried her best to relate to me. Mostly, she worried. As if worrying might send away whatever might be abnormal about me.

It's weird now to think of her constantly looming over me, since she's gone. It hasn't been long since she passed — less than a year. Was it in January or February that she died? My sense of time is off. The past year feels like both a flash and a lifetime, like falling through quicksand in slow motion. I guess that's normal enough; at least, that's what the school psychologist said. Mom got sick and kept getting sicker for a year or so, and then she seemed to be getting better for a while. But she died all the same, suddenly, without any warning. Her heart got bad because of all the chemotherapy, they said. That sometimes happened.

That's when I dug Karen out of a box of old toys and baby clothes in the basement. It's the only physical thing that really reminds me of my mom, for better or worse. Not some picture where everyone's smiling and fake happy. Just something that makes me think of her and the way she was, flaws and all. It's one of the only things I'm bringing to L.A., besides clothes, books and my drawing notebooks. Dad said we had to "pare down."

So now Dad's asking me about troll-doll Karen, just like Mom used to. He's trying to help. But it just brings back memories too sad to think about for long.

"She likes it," I say finally, flatly.

Dad doesn't say anything else for a while. I know he's trying to make things easier for me, but I can't be enthusiastic right now. Of course *he's* excited because we're finally leaving quaint, boring old Galena, leaving behind Mom's death and all the sad people looking at us with big, reddened eyes. He's excited because he's been so down, pacing around the house looking pale and blank as a ghost. The only thing that will cheer him up is to follow the dream he's had since before he met Mom and they had me and decided to stay in their boring hometown. He gets to start writing all the screenplays he's had in his head but couldn't write because he had responsibilities or whatever and try to sell them around town while we live cheaply for a while. I guess he's found a reason to keep going.

Meanwhile, I get to start at a new school in a new state, having lived in the same town my whole life with the same people. So, I'm not excited.

Actually, I'm a *little* bit excited. I have to admit Dad's enthusiasm is sort of contagious. But I can't show it, and it's not exactly a *good* feeling. It's more like something swirling in my stomach, like before you get on a rollercoaster and you know you're either going to have the best time or scream until you feel sick. But I squash this feeling down, disguising it under the sad-girl scowl I've perfected. A sort of empty feeling has taken hold of me over the past few months. It's gotten me through all the shrink visits, the questions from family members, the horrible surprise of having to move away so soon after Mom's death. Going numb also helps me stop missing Mom. But now, with the suddenness of this move, sensation seems to be coming back into my body. I guess after a while, feeling anything, even if it's bad, is better than nothing.

Dad's decided to power through the night. I kind of want to stop and try to pee, but I don't really have to go and don't want to annoy him, so I don't bring it up. I just want to get to wherever it is we're going. The darkness outside is oddly consoling tonight, and the soft, rolling movements our old Chevy makes along the I-15 freeway soothes me until I'm drifting in and out of sleep. I pet Karen's soft, purple hair, imagining it to be a small golden retriever puppy. I'm *so* asking for a puppy once we settle in. *I deserve a puppy*, I think, drifting off as I ponder dog names. *Joni? That sounds right…*

I'm too uncomfortable to sleep for very long. At one point my head slides off the hand I'm sleeping on and my head hits the door handle. I give up after a while. I still don't really know where we are; I crane my neck to look outside, and it's the same as the last time I was awake, just empty darkness for miles around, the moon casting a faint light over the mountains in the distance. A chill goes down my spine.

"Dad, can you turn down the air?" I mutter as I close my eyes again. He doesn't answer. I clutch my arms through my sweatshirt, but the cold still penetrates.

It's completely silent, I realize. I open my eyes. We're moving, but there's a stillness to the air, as if the wheels are spinning in place. Before, the car bumped up and down, up and down, over the long road for miles. Now it teeters back and forth like a boat docked in a harbor.

I start to feel nauseous from the movement. I go to roll down a window and see that my name is still there from where I wrote it before. *Didn't I see it fade away earlier?* I wipe it away with my hand and put my face right up to the window to look out. It's still pitch black out. No light shines down, the moon having almost fully waned. No stars in the sky, either. I pull my sweatshirt over my hand and roll down the window. The air is frigid and feels like cold breath against my skin. *We must be moving at a snail's pace. We'll never get there at this rate. What a slowpoke.*

I stick my head out the window to drink in the desert air. *This is probably unsafe*, I think, but I can't help myself. I gaze downward but I can't even see the road. It's like we're floating.

I pull my head back in, surprised Dad hasn't said anything.

"Dad, where are we ..." I begin, but then I lean forward and realize he isn't there.

I rub my eyes and look around the car in a frenzy, lifting my bookbag, as if my dad could be hiding underneath. I grip the front seats to pull myself forward. The steering wheel turns to and fro, ever so slightly.

"Dad?" I ask again. My voice sounds weak, like I can barely get the words out.

I start to hyperventilate. *This can't be real*, I think, shutting my eyes. *I must have fallen asleep. I'll just wake up now. Any time now.* I open my eyes again to look through the windshield and the road comes into focus, slowly illuminating on either side like a movie-theater aisle. I feel the sensation of the car lurching forward, faster and faster. I see something in the distance. A small, silvery outline. It's getting bigger. Bigger. The butterflies in my stomach are swirling out of control. The silvery outline comes into focus. It's a girl.

"Dad ..." I call out again, weakly, but I can hardly hear my own voice.

The girl's hair undulates in the dead night air, and her translucent arms reach out to either side. She's floating toward us, fast, toward the windshield. We're heading straight for her. We're going to hit her.

"Dad!" I cry out, lurching forward. The seatbelt tightens its grip on me, and I fall back. It's too late. The car swerves and *SMASH*. The sound of crunching plastic is deafening, and the car rolls over a large bump, the seatbelt jabbing into my ribs. We fishtail onto the side of the road, and the car screeches to a halt. I can hear mine and Dad's breathing slowly sync up as we sit unmoving in the car.

"Sweetie!" I hear him say. He whips his head around in the front seat. "Are you OK?" His eyes look wild and red, like he's been crying. But then I realize that he must have fallen asleep.

I squint my eyes and try to remember the last thing I saw. Two glowing eyes, encircled by hair, staring straight into the windshield.

"Dad," I say slowly. "I think we hit something."

"Stay in the car," he says, a little stiffly, as he opens the car door.

I don't do as he says. I can't possibly. I open the door slowly and creep toward the front of the car where Dad is already picking off pieces of fur and blood with his bare hands.

"I think it was a coyote," he says.

I'm horrified and disgusted as Dad continues picking at the car, then rubbing his temples with his bloody fingers.

"Dad, is that, like, healthy?" I ask.

"Well, what am I supposed to do, Rosie?" he asks, pathetically. He stares at me, and his eyes seem to glow like gold in the dark. "We can't go driving around with blood and fur on the front of our car like … like it's some kind of chariot of doom."

He's obviously exhausted, I think. *He's barely making any sense.*

"Dad, did you … fall asleep?"

"I'm fine," he says, pulling himself together. "Rosie, do as I say and get back in the car, please. It's not safe out here."

"What if it's still alive?" I look behind us and see a furry mound breaking up the flat expanse of the road.

"There's nothing we can do now," he says. "Get back in the car."

I look back again and try to remember what it was I saw. But it's like trying to remember someone's name when you know you've lost it. Buckling myself back in, I'm so exhausted that I can't bring myself to worry about Dad falling asleep again. Hopefully, if any good comes of what just happened, it's that it jolted him back awake.

As Dad gets back in the driver's seat, I fall back asleep almost immediately.

*

The next thing I hear is Dad's voice, which sounds gravelly after not speaking for hours. "We're here. Sounds like you had a bad dream."

"Ugh ..." I rub my eyes. They're sore.

Dad opens the car door to reveal a scuzzy-looking motel called the Zorro Inn. A neon-blue arrow blinks irregularly on a large sign in the parking lot, the red outline of a fox's head flickering chaotically beside it.

"The air tastes hot," I say.

Standing in the parking lot, I suddenly remember what happened just before I nodded off again. I spin to look at the front of the car, but I don't see anything. No fur, no blood; just the same old front of the Chevy, only slightly dented.

"Honey?" Dad asks. "Everything OK?"

"How did the car get dented?" I ask.

"Don't you remember? Mom got in that little fender bender when she was sick."

"Oh ... yeah," I say, staring for another second before turning and following him.

I'm in a haze as we walk through the crisp night air. I look around, and all I see are cars zipping through empty space. *Aren't there any trees in California?*

We walk into the less-than-inviting hut that serves as the Zorro's lobby. An Indian girl about my age sits at the front desk, but she immediately runs to fetch someone, probably her dad. I can't figure out why anyone would let someone my age work the front desk of a place like this, but my head hurts and my brain can't wrap itself around much of anything right now.

We walk upstairs quietly an enter a room that smell like old cigarettes. I stare at the creamy looking brown carpet and a painted picture of a fox hanging over the bed while Dad unpacks a few things and talks about our plans. He says we're just out-side of L.A. and we can find a new hotel tomorrow, once we've rested. He's going to spend the next few days looking at apart-ments. I say I'd rather stay and read and watch cable. I know he probably shouldn't leave me alone in strange hotels, but I mut-ter that I need some time alone, and he says he understands. I don't know that he does. But he says it.

As soon as my head hits the pillow, I start drifting in and out of sleep. Dad shuts off the lights.

"Good night, sweetie," he says. "We have a lot of exciting days ahead of us! Get some rest."

"Mmm hmm," I say. Then, "Dad?"

"Yes, honey?"

"What happened to the wolf?"

"What?"

"The coyote," I say, practically delirious. "You said we hit … a coyote?"

"No, sweetie. You just had a bad dream. Go to sleep now."

Lying in bed, my thoughts turn back to the dream I had earlier. Or dreams. I toss and turn, and my whole body feels tight, like I'm bracing myself to hear some terrible news.

Who was she? I think, as I fall into a restless sleep.

CHAPTER 2

We drive up to the beigest building I have ever seen.

In a matter of days, Dad has found us a new place to live. Before we got to L.A., I hadn't even seen that many apartment buildings. Our old house, like many of the houses in Galena, was an aging Victorian home with red bricks and white trim that people would call "quaint." A long set of stone steps led up to the house, and I'd always run as fast as I could to get there, afraid that something was going to come up from behind me. I once told Mom I wanted to move into a nice, new house like I saw on TV.

I guess that's coming back to bite me in the butt now. Our old house seems like a castle in my memory compared to the stucco monstrosity of Valley Village Gardens. I have no idea why it's called that — I can't see any flowers anywhere, just a tiny patch of barely watered grass and a big, old sycamore tree in the front. *This is my new home?* I think. *Oh, shit.*

"It's nice, right?" Dad half-states, half-asks as we drive up.

"Mmm hmm," I say, my lips forming an airtight seal.

A black metal gate yawns open to let our car into the underground parking lot under the building. It feels like a drawbridge, or maybe more like a prison door. There's an older guy standing there with bushy white hair that looks like he's been standing in front of a jet engine. He's wearing a tight green polo shirt and looks like he's from another planet.

"That's Mr. Negrescu," Dad says.

"The landlord?" I ask.

"Yup!"

"Oh, boy." I say. *Oh, shit,* I think again.

Mr. Negrescu, or Mr. N, as he tells me to call him, leads us through a glass door, where we find our tiny mailbox stacked among dozens of others. Up a small set of stained, carpeted stairs, we enter the main courtyard. It's dimly lit by sunlight, quiet and dank. There are three floors, with apartments facing the inside courtyard. I clutch onto my backpack as we creep up an enclosed stairwell that has no lighting.

I'm studying the brown and orange stones cemented into each step — *ochre,* Mom would have corrected me. I'm still looking down when we get to the second floor. We're about to go up another set of stairs, and I yelp when I look up and see the silhouette of an older man standing at his front doorway, behind a metal screen door. He just stands there like a ghost in a bathrobe, balding with gray hair and dark glasses, saying nothing. A tea kettle goes off behind him.

"Honey — hi!" Dad says awkwardly, then waves at the man once he notices him. Dad grabs my hand and we keep walking up, leaving the man standing at his doorway, leaving his tea kettle unattended.

My face must have gone pale. Mr. N says, "That's Mr. Ennis. He lived here since before I bought the place. My wife and I here twenty years! He's harmless though, mama. Don't you worry."

Mr. N walks a few paces ahead of us along an open-air hall lined by another black metal railway overlooking the courtyard. It wouldn't be so bad if everything didn't look so decrepit. The bland stucco is crumbling off the walls, mostly covered by black grime that seems to be dripping off of everything. If Mr. N was trying to make it look like no one had lived in his apartment building for the past twenty years, then mission accomplished.

"This place creeps me out," I say, unable to contain myself.

"Shhh, honey, don't be rude," Dad says. "You haven't seen the apartment yet."

"What did he call me?"

"What? I didn't hear it."

"Mama?"

"I don't know, sweetie. I think they're Greek," he says.

We walk up to a freshly painted white, wooden door — Number 308. Mr. N has to push the door with his shoulder to open it. "It sticks a bit, but what can you do?" he says.

"Um, fix it?" I say under my breath.

We walk inside, and at first I'm actually pleasantly surprised by the musty smell. It's the same smell of the condo we used to rent in South Haven during the summer, during happier times. My parents' friends and their kids would all stay in a row of condos near the lake, where it felt like we'd ride bikes and play all summer, even if in reality it was only a week or so. During those summers, I would always come out of my shell and feel more like a normal kid, with real friends. After a while, though, the trips stopped. My parents stopped talking to a lot of their friends, and I stopped seeing their kids as much.

Once we're inside the apartment, I must look bewildered because Dad takes my hand again and shows me around. There isn't much to see. Two bedrooms and a tiled bathroom. A living room connected to a small, linoleum-floored kitchen with a plain white fridge and a beige, laminate counter where I'm guessing we'll eat a lot of our meals. I rub over a piece of hard, unidentified goo in the mahogany-colored carpet with my shoe.

Gross.

The apartment is dark, and the lights don't seem to work, just like they don't seem to work anywhere in this entire building. Dad yanks open the blinds and lets in a stream of blinding light that seems to only brighten one tiny slice of the living room. I shield my eyes and look out the window. A perfect view of my new dismal little kingdom.

I check out one of the rooms — it's small but cozy, with a window that overlooks the big sycamore tree and the street outside. I can hear cars whirring by. I hope I'll be able to sleep in this place.

"That's your room, honey," Dad says. "You get your own room! And you get the room with the window that looks outside. Isn't it nice?"

"Do we have to share a bathroom?" I ask.

"Oh yeah, sorry about that — but your own room!" he says, gesturing again with his hand as he follows Mr. N into the master bedroom.

He keeps saying "my own room" like I should have expected we would actually sleep in the same room or something. We have to share a bathroom? This is going to suck, big time.

We walk out, and a few doors down, a kid in a striped shirt with brown hair parted down the middle is standing in his doorway and staring at us intensely. As soon as he notices me stare back, he looks down at the ground.

"Oh, honey, this boy looks like he's about your age," Dad says.

I can't believe him. This is literally the worst way he could have possibly begun this interaction.

"Hi," I say to the boy, and wave, even though he's right in front of me. The boy keeps looking down and doesn't say anything.

Guess he's not interested in being friends. God, I'm just as lame as Dad.

"Oh, hello," a woman says, sticking her head out of the doorway. She's about Dad's age, with neat blonde hair streaked with gray and wire-rim glasses resting on her nose. She looks like an old lady in training.

"You must be our new neighbors. Nice to meet you," the woman says. A chunky blue bracelet dangles from her arm as she sticks her hand out to shake Dad's hand. I like her right away.

"Jimmy, say hello to this lovely young lady and her father," she says, prodding the boy. "They're going to be our new neighbors."

"Hi," he says quickly and quietly. His voice and manners make him seem like a little boy, but he's probably only a year or so younger than me. The conversation is so awkward and full of pauses that I feel like I'm not really there and I'm watching it happen on TV.

The boy turns and goes inside. I wonder if I did something to scare him away.

"Jimmy," the woman says with a tone of slight exasperation. There's a slight shake in her voice, like Katherine Hepburn, my mom's favorite actress. She turns back to us, "I'm sorry about that. Jimmy is … a bit different. But he's a nice boy — I'm sure you two will get along. I'm his aunt, Vera. Jimmy lives with me."

Vera says this to both of us, and I appreciate that she isn't talking down to me. My own embarrassment fades, and I feel worse for poor Jimmy.

"That's OK. Jimmy seems great," Dad says cheerily.

"Well, you're welcome to come over any time and play or watch TV. I work from home, so I don't mind watching the kids," Vera says to him.

"Oh, what do you do?" Dad asks.

"I'm a writer."

He's ecstatic. "That's great, I'm a writer too! What do you write?"

"Real estate listings, mostly. Short stories, sometimes." I can tell by Vera's sideways glance that she's not interested in elaborating.

"Dad, don't we have to get our things? Let's go," I say, pulling his sleeve like a child.

"OK, honey," he says, patting me stiffly on the head, twice. "Vera, it was so great to meet you again, to see you. We'll have so much time to talk later about your writing, and my writing, and I'm sure the kids will get along great."

Vera smiles and closes the door.

CHAPTER 3

Dad hires Mr. N's handyman, Alfonso, a nice guy who looks like a redheaded Santa Claus and who lives alone in the building, to help him move the stuff he had shipped to a storage unit before we moved. So, I don't have to do much.

I kind of stand around while Dad and Alfonso do all the heavy lifting, and I try to stay out of the way. I have Karen in my coat pocket, and I reach in on occasion and run my fingers over her marble eyes. After a while, though, I feel restless and decide to explore the rest of the apartment complex.

I walk slowly, taking it all in, not that there's much to take in. Yellowish paint covers old stains and cracks in the walls — it looks like they've been painted over several times. There are black stains of old gum stuck to the ground in a few places, and I wonder if the gum chewer still lives here.

Despite being pretty big, the complex is mostly empty. At one point, a woman walks by with her twin boys. They hardly glance at me, speaking quietly in Chinese before hurrying into their apartment. I don't see any other kids my age around.

I turn a corner and walk into the shared laundry room. It's about 10 square feet, with a single lightbulb dangling in the middle of the room like some grim Christmas ornament. I put my hand over the front of a vending machine and scan its contents. It's mostly laundry detergent, but I spy some Snapple and candy. *They have Whatchamacallits! At least something's looking up here.*

As I stare into the vending machine, the condensation from my mouth spreads out across the glass pane. I start to think about the lakes back home, how they freeze from the outside and then in toward the center. I breathe harder and then rub a hole into the center. *Like that*, I think.

Mom would talk about things like that, how I shouldn't walk onto a frozen lake, even if it looked solid. Dad always said she was being paranoid, that I should be allowed to get into some trouble now and then. I didn't think falling through ice would count as fun childhood trouble; I listened to Mom.

"Your dad's got shit for brains," my Aunt Rita said once, picking me up from the ice rink when Dad forgot to. She was so funny, standing too tall, with her tightly curled black hair and crooked nose making her look exotic for Illinois, like a beautiful witch from another country. I always felt more mature than the other kids, and she was the only one that treated me that way. She had gotten divorced before having kids and then married some weird, quiet guy I didn't really think of as my uncle. Her step-kids were like little rats, running around aimlessly. I'd try to play with them when I was younger, but there was no sense of imagination to their games, so I'd usually just bug Aunt Rita and ask her questions about R-rated movies I wanted to see and family secrets — "adult stuff" that excited me.

I miss Aunt Rita. We didn't get the chance to say bye before we left. Things were strained between Dad and Mom's family after she died, but still. Dad says we'll call later and go back and visit, but I'm not holding my breath. Vera reminds me a little bit of Aunt Rita.

It suddenly occurs to me that I've been standing in an empty laundry room for a while for no real reason. Not that there's really anywhere to go, but I've been lost in my thoughts again and haven't been paying attention to how the move's going. I walk out of the laundry room and turn the corner, heading toward the parking garage. I peek my head in, but I don't see Dad or

Alfonso anywhere.

"Dad?" I call out. I don't hear anything except my own voice ping-ponging off the floor and ceilings. I want to call to him again, but I don't want to embarrass myself in case anyone can hear me. I stand there a minute longer, staring into the almost empty parking garage and listening for anyone or anything, but all I see is a handful of beat-up cars. *He must be upstairs now*, I think. *Thanks for leaving me alone, Dad.*

I walk back inside. Despite it being broad daylight outside, the dim courtyard lets little light in. *Seriously, can't these people afford to put in a lamp or two?*

I walk toward the stairs and ascend slowly, one step at a time. On the second floor, I hold my breath as I approach Mr. Ennis' door. *Don't look*, I think. *He might be standing there like a weirdo again. Just keep walking.* But I can't help myself. I turn my head as I reach the door.

He's standing there again, like before, with his bathrobe open and only a tank top and pajama pants on underneath. He's leaning on a cane and peering through those dark glasses right at me. I turn and run the rest of the way up the stairs and along the hallway. I grab at the doorknob of our apartment, and thankfully it's unlocked. I enter and shut the door quickly behind me.

Breathing heavily, I look around at the apartment, which is full of boxes and a dusty, brown corduroy couch Mr. N donated to us. *There's no one here.*

Suddenly, I see a rush of movement from behind the boxes. I scream.

"There you are, princess!" Dad says, suddenly emerging.

"I think we scared the princesa," Alfonso says, coming in from the hallway.

"Oh. Sorry," I say. "I didn't see you. I was … exploring."

"That's fine," Dad says. "Get to know your new home. Alfonso and I will take care of everything."

I try to shake off the weirdness of Mr. Ennis and sit cross-legged on the carpet to start peeling the tape off of one of my boxes. I guess it's nice that Dad even noticed I was gone. I smile at him when he looks at me as he's putting down two heavy boxes at once. I can see how much it means to him, and that makes me feel better, too.

Eventually, Dad and Alfonso leave to take care of more moving-in details. Ten, maybe fifteen minutes pass before I realize they left the door wide open as I sit on the floor, alone. *So much for caring about what happens to me*, I think.

I shut the door and then walk around the apartment with Karen in hand. I make us a little space among the boxes and lie on the carpet in my new room, stroking her hair and staring at the ceiling. *I don't feel like unpacking right now*, I think. *Maybe I'll find my pads and pencils and sketch something.*

I sit up and start to open a box of my stuff with a pair of scissors. My mind wanders to when we moved into our old house. I was about six, and I distinctly remember opening boxes with an X-Acto knife. It's no surprise that I managed to cut myself — now, my right hand caresses a faint, zigzagging scar on my left middle finger that looks like a little lightning bolt. "It just means you're a firecracker," Dad would say of the scar, which I didn't really get — it looked like lightning, not a firecracker.

I get up and pace back and forth across the short hallway, imagining my new life. But everything feels too unreal. I try to imagine what my friends might look like. I imagine playing tag with a blonde girl in a long pink dress, in a plain white house, but I can't see her face. It seems cartoonish. I can't imagine anything real.

I'm lying on the ground again when I hear a quick chafing sound.

I sit up fast. *It has to be the door*, I think. But the noise is weird. It sounds like someone dragging themselves along the ground.

"Dad?" I call out into the empty apartment. Nothing.

I hear another sound. This time, it's a loud thump and a swish, like someone dropping a sack of dirty clothes and dragging it along the carpet. The hairs on the back of my neck stand up. It's quiet again. But I feel like I'm not alone.

I get up and walk back through the apartment hallway slowly, my fingers gliding along the walls, hoping to see my dad and Alfonso when I enter the main room. But it's just the same piles of boxes. I don't see them or anyone.

This is an old building, I tell myself. *There's gonna be a lot of weird noises.*

"It's probably the laundry or something," I say out loud, awkwardly, as if to keep myself company. I've never minded being alone; actually, I prefer it most of the time. But I've never liked the dark. The evening has started to darken, and the lights in our apartment aren't working yet. I breathe out deeply, as if warding something off. The room feels cold and suffocating as I stand there in a circle of boxes. It feels like they could close in on me at any second.

I draw the shades fully open. It doesn't seem to make a difference; hardly any light pours through, mostly shining on one spot on the floor.

Should I go outside? What if that noise came from outside? It sounded so close. Did I imagine it?

I'm frozen, trying to calm my mind. It's gotten dark enough in here that I can see light underneath the doorway. The sound of something dragging around seems to echo from every wall. I spin around, but all I see are stacks of boxes towering over me. Suddenly, I hear a high-pitched laugh that seems to come from just outside. Shadows interrupt the light under the door. The door flings open. I turn and scream.

"Honey! What's wrong?"

"I think we scared the princesa again," Alfonso says.

"Sorry!" I say, and run back to my room.

I shut the door behind me. I don't know what to feel. Mostly, I feel annoyed. They keep leaving me alone in this strange place, and I'm getting sick of this "princesa" business.

I come out again a few minutes later.

"You OK?" Dad asks.

"I'm fine," I say.

Alfonso looks at me, puzzled. His hands are full. "Do you have a place you want to put your bookcase? Maybe for your dollies?" he asks me.

"No, whatever, wherever is fine," I say, walking quickly back into my new room. I try to clear my mind and catch my breath.

I try to focus on what I can do to decorate my room, but my mind is as blank as the walls surrounding me. I gaze at them, trying to imagine anything but that high-pitched laugh I heard. *What is this feeling? There's nothing strange here, right?* But I close my eyes and it feels like the walls are closing in around me. Nothing feels right.

CHAPTER 4

I'm settling into my new home, but I can't deny that the place majorly gives me the creeps. I can't get comfortable. It's summer and sweltering, so we open the windows, but it doesn't seem to help. The air conditioning is supposed to be getting fixed, but Alfonso has gone to visit his family in Mexico. At this rate, we'll have A/C by December.

More than the heat, though, it's a feeling that bothers me. I can only pass off the strange noises as my imagination for so long. The lighting never seems to light up much of anything. The place feels fake, like the movie version of an apartment building. I can't help but think of what Mom would say. "What a dump!" she'd say, imitating Elizabeth Taylor in *Who's Afraid of Virginia Wolf?* — another of her favorite actresses. She was always good at diffusing Dad's crazy ideas, which would send him off into a sulk. Without her, there was no one to do that.

I think of her as I'm organizing the bathroom, a task I volunteer for to spare us both the embarrassment of him dealing with my "lady things". My hand picks out a small, green medicine bottle from the box — one of Mom's. I thought all of these had been tossed out. I jiggle the remaining pills and stare at it a while. I know I should toss it, but and decide to stuff it in one of the drawers. It brings back sad memories, but they're memories I'd like to keep anyway.

I'm putting it away when I see the shower curtain rustle behind me in the mirror. Instinctively, my head whips around, but I don't see anything out of the ordinary. The shower curtain just sits there, powder blue and unmoving.

"Dad?" I call out.

"Yeah, honey?" he answers from his bedroom. "Did you find my toothbrush?"

"Uh huh," I say, not thinking about his question. I don't say anything more. I just want to know he's nearby. I look back at the mirror. My face looks pale and hollow. I can almost hear Mom saying to me, "You look like you've seen a ghost."

Suddenly, everything feels too quiet. *I know I saw it move. There's only one way to find out.*

I creep toward the shower, then hesitate. *What if there's a rat or a spider in there? Or something else …*

I pull back the curtain quickly.

"Aha!" I say.

"What is it, Rosie?" Dad calls from the other room.

"Nothing," I say, returning to the box. I realize the window's been open the whole time. *Just the breeze, Rosie. No big deal.*

Later on, though, I'm not so sure. I'm in the kitchen, taking dishes out from a box, many of which are broken. *I wish Dad would take his car in*, I think, recalling the bumpy ride from Illinois. I put the empty shards in the trash, careful not to cut myself. I can't help but run my finger over the lightning-bolt scar on my middle finger, reminding myself to not be such a klutz.

I wash the surviving dishes and run the new sponge slowly over the faint red rings that interlock and surround the plates. To me, they've always looked like bloody vines closing in on whatever food I'm eating. I think they're just supposed to be a pretty design, though. *What's wrong with you, Rosie?*

I've never minded doing the dishes. Dad won't do them, anyway.

But these were Mom's favorites. They got them as a wedding gift, right before I was born, and she always said they reminded her of "the best times." I imagine her standing and cradling me in the kitchen while Dad types away furiously in the dining room, shouting ideas to her. I'm kind of cradling this plate, too, when Dad tugs on my shirt from behind. He startles me so badly that I drop the plate onto the floor, where it shatters.

"Shit!" I say. "Dad, you scared—"

"Honey! Don't swear, please," Dad says. His voice is still coming from the bedroom.

I scan the living room and realize I'm alone. After another moment, I get down on my hands and knees and scoop up the pieces quickly.

"What happened?" Dad says, coming into the room.

"Dad," I begin. I look down at the rest of the shattered pieces on the tiled floor. "Sorry. I dropped a plate."

"Rosie!" he says, before calming down. "That's OK, honey. Just try to be careful, or we'll never get this all done."

He walks back toward the bedroom, leaving me kneeling on the floor over the broken pieces.

"Thanks for helping, Dad," I say under my breath. *I wonder if he noticed which plate I broke. I hope not.*

I'm washing my hands when I notice they're bleeding. All those little shards I picked up so hastily. My hands are shaking, too. *What happened to make me drop that plate?*

Just another creepy thing that you're probably imagining, Rosie, I tell myself. *No need to freak out.*

CHAPTER 5

That night, I stay up late in front of the TV. With the windows open to keep cool, I can hear cars whizzing by like racecars, the occasional sirens and faint yelling. Dad says I'll still be able to go to a nice school on the other side of the freeway, but he won't let me venture far from the complex by myself.

I flip back and forth between David Letterman and MTV as "Alternative Nation" is just starting. We can't really afford cable, but after I complained enough times, Dad finally relented.

Nuzzling into our dusty couch, I find myself drifting in and out of sleep shortly after midnight. As I trudge off to bed, the noise of cars has died down to barely a whisper. I'm exhausted at this point, but I still can't quite fall asleep. I stare at the ceiling and watch the shadows of the sycamore tree shake, moving up and down on the closet door.

I try to think about Mom before I fall asleep, in the hope of seeing her in my dreams. I imagine her kissing me on the cheek and pulling up the blanket to my chin, like she did when I was younger. But she's never there. Even when I have nice dreams, about growing up and the good times we had on vacation, she's nowhere to be found.

I've had the same dream several times since Mom died. I'm in the yard, playing in the dirt like I would have as a kid. When I realize no one else is around, I go looking for Mom, up the long set of stone steps leading to the house. I look for her everywhere in a labyrinthine approximation of our old house. The walls are blindingly white. Light streams in unnaturally bright from the windows. I walk upward in an endless spiral, up three, four, five floors, but it's just the same space, the same rooms and hallways but laid out differently. Sometimes, I finally see the right hallway. I walk down it toward my parents' bedroom, but the door is shut fast, so I turn around and descend the staircases once again. Only they never stop. I'm huffing and look up and down, and it's endless stairs as far as the eye can see. I decide to start taking them two at a time until I trip and go tumbling down, down, down, farther and farther until I wake up.

Tonight, I have this same dream. But this time, it's slightly different. I end up at the bedroom, but this time, the handle jiggles as if it's about to open. It sounds like someone is on the other side, pushing with all of their weight to get out. I step back and try to call out Mom's name, but no sound comes out. I keep calling and calling until I wake myself up. I sit up, relieved to be back in my bed.

Once I fall back asleep, I just dream that I'm a cast member on "The Real World." It's a lot nicer of a dream, although I'm not so sure I'd want that in real life. Puck seems like a jerk.

*

Dad seems to be taking to our new life well. During the day he writes furiously, yelling at himself or verbally patting himself on the back for every crappy idea that pops into his head. "Shit! Danny boy, get it together," he'll say to no one in particular. He goes by Dan but calls himself Danny boy, like a child. It's embarrassing.

He can't really tolerate my restlessness when he's working. "Honey, stop circling," he tells me one ordinary summer afternoon. "Daddy's trying to get some very important work done. Why don't you see if Vera and Johnny are around, hmm? Watch some TV over there."

We've met two people in this dumb building, and he can't even re-

member their names right.

"Sure, Dad."

I oblige and knock on Jimmy's door — number 304, just a few down from ours.

Vera's wonderfully uncombed head of hair pokes out and she smiles down at me. "Come in, lovey," she says, beckoning with her long fingers. I love that she calls me that — just like the Howells on "Gilligan's Island."

The kitchen smells like boiling cabbage or some such vegetable. It's not a good smell, but it's somehow comforting. The radio is on, and "Low" by Cracker is playing.

"Oh, I like this song!" I say.

"Isn't it great?" Vera says. "Well, Jimmy's just watching cartoons in the other room if you want to join him. Would you like a glass of water?"

"Sure, thanks, Mrs. Mason."

"Oh, lovey, I'm no 'missus.' Never been married. Vera's fine."

"OK. Sorry, Vera."

"No need to be sorry," she says, smiling faintly and patting my head. The thrill of adulthood quickly leaves me.

Vera and Jimmy's place looks just like ours, only a mirror image and lived in. There are dreamcatchers over every door, and paintings of flowers, and an older-looking one of a kid that almost looks like Jimmy but dressed in an old timey blue satin outfit, holding a cat. I hunker down next to Jimmy, who's watching "Rugrats."

"Jimmy, why don't you ask Rosie what she wants to watch?" Vera asks.

"Do you like 'Rugrats'?" Jimmy asks.

"Not really. I mean, I used to when I was younger," I reply. "I usually just watch MTV or something." I instantly regret this response because I actually love "Rugrats," and I feel bad at assuming Jimmy's allowed to watch MTV.

"Oh, that's fine. Jimmy loves MTV," Vera says, grabbing the remote and flipping the channel. Jimmy moans quietly in protest but becomes transfixed by writhing, half-naked bodies on "MTV Beach House."

"Hey y'all!" says a beautiful blonde woman in a bikini top holding a microphone. "We've got the hottest tunes — and the hottest bods — all summer long! Coming up, we've got videos by TLC, The Cranberries…"

Jimmy stares at the screen wide-eyed. I'm too embarrassed to speak. Thankfully, Vera leaves the room.

After about an hour of music videos and vapid beach people, I wander to the kitchen. Vera is sitting quietly, not doing much of anything.

"I just wanted more water," I say.

"Oh, that's fine, lovey. Grab whatever you like. There's some soda in the fridge as well."

"OK, thanks, I might have one. My dad always forgets to buy groceries."

Vera shifts and holds her hand near her face as if she's about to smoke an imaginary cigarette. I've seen Dad do it. He used to smoke. "It's a tough thing raising a child on your own. How're you and your dad holding up?"

"We're fine. He works mostly, during the day. He's writing something. He won't show it to me though. I don't know if it's any good." The words tumble out of me, and I clam up about it before I say anything else weird. "Did … you paint these?" I ask about a painting of white lillies on the kitchen wall.

"Yes, a long time ago," she says, chuckling. "I don't find as much time to paint anymore. How about you? Do you like to draw?"

"Yeah!" I say. "I mean, how did you know?"

"Us artists just recognize each other," she says, smiling. I smile back, although I dread her asking to see some of my crappy drawings. Thankfully, she doesn't. I study the painting of lilies further. My eyes focus on the bright white of the petals, as I notice two small, glowing yellow eyes in the dark background of the painting. *Who is that?*

"Well, you're welcome here any time," she says, bringing my attention back. "I know Jimmy's not much of a talker, but he's a good kid. And you can always talk to me too. Really, I don't mind. I like the company."

"Thanks, Vera." I silently plan to come over as often as I can that summer.

*

That night I lie down, exhausted, and beg myself to relax and get to sleep. I stare at the sycamore outside my window. I think about Mom, the feel of the soft blanket against my skin. I think about the summers we spent on Lake Michigan. It seems to be working: I feel myself drifting off.

I start to see little yellow lights dancing inside my eyelids, the kind you see when you rub your eyes. Slowly, I open my eyes. A drop of sweat trickles down my forehead. I have no idea what time it is or how long I've been asleep. I do this thing I do when I first wake up, where I try to make a fist but can't. I reach over to pull the window open. Wincing at its weight, I give up and lay back down. I stare at my feet, and my eyes blur. Just beyond my gaze, at the closet door, a faint white outline comes into focus.

I sit up in my bed and throw the blanket off of me. I try to make sense of what I'm seeing.

"It's just your jacket on the chair," I whisper to myself.

But it's not that. I can see the chair over by my desk, and it's empty.

I tell myself it's just the shadows of the tree outside the window. But this is different. The silhouette is standing there, plain as day. It's not a reflection or an optical illusion. Outside, the wind has gone still, and the sycamore casts no shadow.

I've felt this presence before — in the kitchen, in the bathroom, the way it's felt like someone has been following me, watching me as I walk around the building. It's like when you feel someone staring at you, or sense them walking up behind you before you even hear them. I can almost feel it at my throat, curling around my neck as my breath quickens.

I grab the blanket and pull it over my mouth. The figure doesn't move. I cover my face for a moment and pull it down slowly. *It's still there.* A soft, star-shaped shadow with a faint white outline. *There's no reason for it to be there, but it's there. This has to be a dream.*

I start to get up, moving slowly toward the closet door. The figure grows fainter the closer I get. My heart beats faster and faster, but I can't stop moving toward it. *I need to know what this is.*

My hand reaches out. *There — I can almost touch it!*

The figure fades into nothing as my fingers brush against the closet door. I stand there for a minute, dumbfounded. Then I jump back into bed and pull the blankets over me. I can't stop shaking, even in this heat. *Whatever it is I've been seeing, it's getting closer to me.*

CHAPTER 6

I try to forget about what I saw in my room, but suddenly watching reruns of "I Love Lucy" until "Andy Griffith" all day long has lost its appeal.

What is going on, here? Is this place really haunted? I could tell Dad or even Mr. N, but they'd probably just laugh at me.

The other day, coming home from a later-than-usual Thursday evening trip with Dad to Target to stock up on ramen and spaghetti, Mr. Ennis' door was closed. I don't think I'd actually ever seen it closed before. I hurried past it as usual, but as I did, I noticed there was a small, white sign with a few words scrawled across it hanging on his door. I didn't stop to look and see what it says, but I haven't stopped thinking about it.

Today, with the strangeness I've experienced lately weighing on me, I decide it's time to get over my fear of Mr. Ennis and see what's written on his door.

Mr. Ennis' front door is open again, with just the screen door closed, but I have a plan. I'll walk past quickly to see if he's standing there like usual. If the screen door is closed and he's in his recliner, watching TV as he often does, I'll creep from upstairs and move the front door slightly to read the sign. With that dark apartment and those dark glasses, he'll never notice me.

I shuffle by his front door, quickly enough to not draw any attention but slowly enough to see that him sitting in his recliner. He's vigorously eating something out of a bowl and watching

TV. Perfect timing.

I hang around downstairs for a minute, trying to look inconspicuous, then I walk back up to our apartment and open the door. Dad's sitting at the counter, clanking away on his typewriter. He's muttering to himself and doesn't seem to hear me. I stand and stare at him for a minute before quietly shutting the door again.

Back outside, I walk softly, hanging close to the wall. It's an oddly gray day for the California summer, and there's barely a sound, other than the occasional soft humming of an airplane making its landing into Burbank Airport.

I start to creep sideways down the stairwell, hugging the wall as if I were one of those suction-cupped toys on a car window. I stop when I'm a few feet from Mr. Ennis' door and involuntarily clench my hands into fists. *What am I doing? What if he sees me?*

Nothing bad's gonna happen, Rosie. Besides, there's not much else going on around here.

I'm right by the doorway now. There's no point in going back. I reach over and move the door outward just an inch. There's no way to see the sign from here. I move the door a few more inches, slowly. I can see the white piece of paper, but I can't read the writing in the darkness of the shadow of the door. I push a little harder, and my fingers glide across the door, pushing it harder than I meant to. *Crap!*

My eyes dart over the words as the door hits the frame. My heart's pounding. I'm not sure what I was expecting, but it's definitely not what I end up seeing. It says:

> ROOM OF DESPAIR
>
> Lawyers stole my home and left me
> to die. They poisoned my wife also.
>   Now I am doomed. The hands that

pull to the earth

The sign is about a head above me. It must be some sick joke I don't understand. I'm frozen.

Now I can see Mr. Ennis emerging. His fingers reach around the door and he swings around to stare straight at me. He takes off his dark glasses, and his pure black pupils stare straight through me. I scream, but it's too late. He yanks my arm, a bloodcurdling growl coming from his cigar-stained mouth, and he laughs as he pulls me into his apartment and shuts the door.

My back is against the door. I'm breathing heavily.

"Honey!" Dad says. "Don't slam the door. What do you need?"

"Huh?" I say, panting.

As if gliding on air, my feet have carried me up the stairs and back into our apartment before I've even realized what has happened ... which, it seems, is nothing.

Dad turns back to his typewriter and gets back to work. On my tippy toes, I can't see much through the peephole, so I open the door slowly, wide enough to see down the stairs.

Mr. Ennis' door is still half open. I sit on the floor and keep peering out through the crack in the doorway.

A few minutes later, he emerges. It's the same as usual — he's in a dingy white tank top and pajama pants, and his hair looks slept on. I can't make out his features, although this is the most of him I've seen so far. He hobbles out of the apartment and looks around quickly before going back inside and shutting the door behind him.

I've been on my hands and knees watching. Now I get up and close the door.

When I turn around, Dad is right there, looking at me. "What's gotten into you, Rosie?"

I tell Dad about the sign.

"He's harmless, Rosie," is Dad's reply. "Mr. N said so."

"Dad, I don't think we should take his word for it. That guy is really weird."

"He's probably a little bit sick in the head, honey. Just don't bother him and leave him be, OK? Stay away from him."

CHAPTER 7

Stone Temple Pilots' "Plush" is playing on my tape deck and I'm sinking into the couch. It's on tape because we can't afford CDs. Dad let me buy a few tapes from Target while we went out for toilet paper and microwave dinners. As I'm listening, I open the cassette sleeve and look at Scott Weiland's sinewy body. He looks menacing in the video for "Sex Type Thing," but he's cute in "Plush," with his rose-red dyed hair. I'd love to dye my hair like that one day. Mom would never let me do something like that, but Dad would.

"Doesn't he sound like that other singer you like? Pearl Jam?" Dad asks from the kitchen counter.

"Pearl Jam isn't a guy, Dad. It's a band. No, they don't sound the same. Pearl Jam suck."

"I like that song we heard on the way home. 'Jeremy spoke in class today…'" he sings in a fake deep voice.

I laugh even though he's being lame. He's in a good mood, for once. He says he finished writing something. *Thank God.*

Dad says he's going out to celebrate his "success." He's convinced one of the few people knows in L.A. to meet him for a drink. This means I'll be spending the evening at Vera and Jimmy's.

This turns out to be a lot more fun than I would have imagined. I ask Vera if she has any music, and she shows me and Jimmy her record collection. Neil Young, Creedence Clearwater Revival, The Beatles … at least I know the last one. She plays us a little bit of Led Zeppelin, a song called "When the Levee Breaks," and

I love it immediately. Jimmy waves his fists around in a sort of maraca dance on the bed in Vera's room and I can't help but laugh. I stifle it and look apologetically at Vera. She smiles to let me know it's OK.

The phone rings. Immediately, Vera's tone becomes serious and she kicks us out of her room, pulling the phone into the bedroom and shutting the door.

We're lying on the carpet watching old sitcoms — "Cheers" and "Mary Tyler Moore." I don't think Jimmy likes them much, but I insist on watching.

"Why are we watching this?" Jimmy asks.

"I dunno, I just like it. They remind me of my mom," I blurt out.

"Oh," Jimmy says. "Moms."

"Yeah ..." I say.

"Aunt Vera was talking to my mom."

"Oh, I thought ... I didn't know."

"I don't see her that much."

"Sorry, Jimmy."

"Is your mom ... gone?"

Gone. I let that word bounce around my skull for a moment. It's the easiest way I can think of describing it, I guess. "Yeah," is all I can say.

We sit in silence a minute. I try to get Jimmy to focus on "Mary Tyler Moore."

"She's trying to prove herself," I tell Jimmy. "All the guys in the office like her, but they pretend they don't because she's a woman working in their office, and they don't like that."

Jimmy cradles his head in his hands like a baby, rocking back and forth. His blue eyes dart from the TV to the corners of the room. His hair is standing up in brown streaks. He's actually kind of cute, but not, like, Scott Weiland cute — more like a little brother.

"Why are they all old?" he asks.

"They're not old, that's just how people looked in the '70s."

"This is boring!" he says, rolling over. "I wanna play tag."

"We can't play tag. It's nighttime, and there's only two of us. Your aunt won't let us go."

"It's OK!" Jimmy gets up, opens the front door, walks out and immediately bolts down the hall. The thing is, Jimmy doesn't really do what anyone tells him to do.

"Shit," I say. I look outside, and Jimmy's halfway across the third floor. "OK, just stay on this floor!" I shout at him.

"Why?" he asks, turning. "I'm gonna go to the bottom floor. You have to catch me!"

This building and the people in it are weird enough during the day. Nighttime is another story. I'm not about to go crawling around in the dark recesses of our building looking for Jimmy, with Mr. Ennis lurking around.

"No!" I shout, but Jimmy can't hear me. I stand frozen outside the apartment for a minute. I think about telling Vera, but she's still on the phone, with the telephone cord trailing under her bedroom door. Now I've waited too long and I'm going to have to find Jimmy.

I close the apartment door, steel myself and run downstairs, avoiding looking at Mr. Ennis' door.

"Why is it so dark down here?" I say out loud, trying not to sound scared. I run aimlessly, looking for Jimmy. I don't even see the three shadowy figures until it's too late, and I almost crash into them.

"Ahh!" I yell and stop. The Asian mom stands before me, wide-eyed and holding a paper bag full of groceries. Her twin sons clutch on to her.

"Sorry!" I say, catching my breath.

"It's OK," she says in perfect English. I don't know why I was expecting anything different. It bothers me that I was.

"You guys wanna play?" she asks her kids.

But they just clutch on to her even tighter and shake their heads underneath their red raincoats.

"Just be careful," she says to me, and I nod. I turn around to see where Jimmy ran off to. A few seconds later, I see the light of the family's apartment turn off. Darkness and silence again.

I hear a faint, high-pitched sound, like someone trying not to giggle, coming from underneath the stairwell. "Jimmy, this is so stupid. We're too old for this!" I shout, embarrassed. "Jimmy, where are you?"

I trudge back toward the stairwell, shaking my head. *He's gotta be hiding underneath. But it's so dark under there …*

"OK, Jimmy, I found you," I say, standing beside by the stairs. I hear the giggle again, slightly higher pitched than Jimmy's normal voice. *He's acting like such a little kid.* "Jimmy, come out!" I call into the space, annoyed.

Nothing — other than my voice echoing into the space below the stairs, reverberating as if it went on for miles. "Jimmy, come out, Jimmy, come out …" it rings out, as if mocking me.

I listen closely, but all I hear is a low humming sound that always seems to be just below the surface in this building, every time you stop to pay attention to it. I can feel heat radiating from under the stairs, coming out in waves.

"I win!"

The voice is coming from above me. I back up and look upward to see Jimmy standing on the third floor, his long arms dangling over the railing. He looks down at me, puzzled, and I turn and hustle up the stairs.

I can feel it again. The sensation of something at my back. I run past Mr. Ennis' apartment and hear the knob turning as I approach, and I double my speed, running into Jimmy at the top of the stairs.

"Ugh!" I cry out as I land on my stomach, knocking the wind out of me. I look back. No one's there, of course. Jimmy laughs.

"It's not funny!" I yell at him. "Stop it! I heard you laughing at me earlier."

"I was just here. I was waiting for you," he says softly.

Jimmy helps me up. I wince as I step onto my ankle. But I feel bad for yelling at Jimmy and embarrassed about falling.

"Sorry," I say. "I heard someone giggling."

Jimmy looks at me silently.

"It was under the stairs," I say, motioning behind me. "Maybe it was a cat or something."

"I have cats!" a voice says.

Jimmy and I look up to see an elderly, short-haired woman in a ratty nightrobe standing at the doorway of apartment 302. She grins at us, then continues, "Two of them. Their names are Coco and Peanut. They are very nice little cats! Would you like to meet them?"

"Oh," I say. I look over at Jimmy, but he's looking down and playing with his thumbs. "That's OK. Um, I think one of them got out."

She stares back at us and blinks a couple of times, still smiling. Her grin stretches across her face, as if etched there.

"No. Coco and Peanut are right here." She reaches down and picks up a fat orange tabby that she can barely support. Coco (or Peanut) emits a low half-growl, half-purr that doesn't sound anything like what I heard earlier. "Do you want to say hi, Coco?"

"That's OK, Mrs. Lieberman," Jimmy suddenly says. He grabs my hand and we walk back to his apartment.

"Coco is short for Coconut," Mrs. Lieberman says behind us. Jimmy starts giggling.

"That's Mrs. Lieberman," he informs me. "She's really old."

"I figured that out," I say.

We go back inside. Vera's off the phone but seems unaware of our venturing out. I try to pass off my hobbling, but soon it becomes obvious. To my surprise, Vera isn't mad, though. She quickly fashions a cold compress out of a freezer bag, ice and a dishrag, and instructs me to sit with my leg up while we watch "M*A*S*H". I don't like "M*A*S*H" much, but I don't say anything, and I'm not paying attention anyway. I doze off and on, wondering, *What did I hear earlier? Was it anything at all?*

CHAPTER 8

On another summer Wednesday, Dad's being grumpy and trying to get through some work, so I'm out walking around the apartment complex. I'm distracted by a bad feeling in the pit of my stomach, something I've been ignoring for a while. The feeling that something terrible is going to happen and I can't do anything to stop it.

Could I just nervous about school starting? No, it's something else. The sound under the stairs. The vision in my bedroom. They must be connected somehow.

I'm about to turn the corner to head to the stairs leading down to the second floor, lost in thought, when I hear a jingling sound. I stop at the corner and peer around, but I don't see anyone.

I look over the edge of the railing, thinking it might be the sound of a pet's collar. There are a couple of small dogs in the complex, even though we're not supposed to have them. I scan the area, but all I see is the solitary potted birds of paradise reaching up from the center of the courtyard, its exotic colors hilariously out of place in the drab building.

I continue walking until I'm at apartment 301, at the top of the stairs that lead down to the second floor. There are keys hanging from the door. It takes me a minute to realize how strange it is that the keys have been left there, and that they're moving as if someone let them go only moments ago.

A shiver goes down my spine, and not the good kind, like when that Lisa Loeb song comes on the radio. But I try to make sense of it. Someone must have gone inside and left their keys in the door.

I'm not sure why, but I take the keys out of the door. Against my better judgment, I decide to try to return them to their owner.

I knock on the door and wait. There's no answer. *I could just use these keys to get in and leave them on the nearest table or something,* I think. Mom would say that would be the right thing to do. She'd also tell me not to talk to strangers or wander into random apartments. That's something Dad would do.

I stand there with the two sides of my brain battling it out for a minute. I knock on the door again. No one answers.

Looks like the bored and curious side wins today.

I unlock the door and open it slightly. Inside, the front room looks a lot like ours, only it's painted a slightly more "off" version of off-white. And it's totally empty. The apartment smells like paint. And something else … something I can't put my finger on.

I look behind me, but it's as dead as always in Valley Village Gardens. So, I take a step inside.

I walk into the kitchen. It's mostly the same as ours. The linoleum on the floor is older and has a red patterning. I bend over to look more closely.

I reach my hand down to touch it. It's not a pattern—it's wet.

Blood? My heart beats faster as I raise my fingers to my face.

Actually, it smells like tomato sauce.

As I stand up, I notice movement out of the corner of my eye. My head whips around. I stare down the hallway to what would be my room, if this were our apartment. Except the hallway stretches farther down. The door to the room is cracked open. As I'm staring, the door closes and clicks softly, as if someone on the other side wants privacy. Then, as slowly as it closed, it opens up again.

"It's just the wind, Rosie," I say out loud. *Oh crap, what if there is something there, and what if it heard me?*

I bolt out of the kitchen and out of the apartment, then close the door behind me. I realize the keys are still in my hand, but there's no way in hell I'm going back in there right now, so I try to put them back in the door — but they won't go back in this time. I jiggle the key for a minute, but it's no use. *Crap, now what do I do?* I wonder if I should tell Mr. N. But I just want to get out of there, so I stuff the keys into my pocket and walk downstairs quickly.

Scuttling along the second floor, I'm distracted and forget my usual fixation on Mr. Ennis, so I'm not thinking about him as I pass his open door and through a wave of cigar smoke. It catches me off guard, and I accidentally inhale deeply, forcing me to stop and cough.

I hear a man's voice say softly, "Sorry." The voice doesn't sound apologetic. It's more of a quiet statement, with no real emotion behind it. It comes from some empty place.

I look to my right slowly. The front door's open like usual, and Mr. Ennis is standing there, cigar smoke pouring out of the screen door. I can't see him through the darkness of his apartment and the cloud of smoke he's breathing out, but I swear that I can feel his eyes piercing through the smoke, boring holes right through me.

I shake my head and run as fast as I can down the rest of the stairs. I trip on the bottom two steps and spill into the courtyard.

I sense movement behind me. Two feet in slippers approach before I can get up. *He's here!*

No, these are women's slippers. They're sequined.

"Oopsie," a heavily accented voice says. "Don't run down the stairs or you fall and hurt yourself bad!"

A chubby hand with bright red nails and dangling bracelets reaches down. I take it and lift my head to see a plump, curly-haired woman in a blue floral dress standing in front of me. "I'm Elena — Mrs. Negrescu," she says. "You just move in with your dad?"

"Yeah," I say, getting up. "Sorry I was running."

"No problem. You two settle in OK?"

"Yeah, we're OK." I hesitate. "Uh, I think someone left their keys in the door upstairs," I say, dusting off my Mudd Jeans. "Apartment 301."

"Oh, OK! Maybe my husband was doing some work in there. No one lives there now. I'll tell him. Thank you, girl. What's your name?"

"Rosie."

"Thank you, Rosie. We live in number 101. Come over any time you want, I'll make you really good tea. You like tea?"

"I don't know."

She laughs. "You never had tea, girl? OK, you come over sometime and have some tea. And be careful running around here. You never know what can happen."

I wonder what she means by that. But I realize something may just have been lost in translation. "OK, sorry, Mrs. N."

"No problem!" she says, waving her hand as if swatting a fly. "You just call me Elena, mama."

"OK, Elena."

She shuffles upstairs in her sequined slippers. I stand there in the courtyard, rubbing my right knee. "No smoking in here!" I hear her tell Mr. Ennis. "How many times do I have to tell you? Go outside if you want to smoke." He mutters a few words in response, but I can't hear what he says, and she continues upstairs. *I'm so stupid,* I think to myself. *There's nothing to be afraid of around here.*

I turn to walk upstairs, but then I hear the jingling again, the same as before. A meowing sound startles me so badly that I flip around immediately, scanning the courtyard. Nothing there. I turn around to see a dark shape slink under the stairwell.

"Ugh, it was just a stupid cat the whole time," I say to myself.

I peer under the stairs, hoping to find it and return it to Mrs. Lieberman. It's impossibly dark under there, even though it's already late morning.

"God ... gross," I say as I pull spider webs off my face. I hate spiders, but I put that aside for the moment. *Where the heck is this cat?* "Here, kitty kitty," I say. "Coco? ... Peanut?"

Underneath the stairs, I move forward through a darkened space that seems larger than it could possibly be from the outside. I reach a closed door with light pouring through two horizontal slits in it. *There's no way a cat could have gone in there. What's down here? It must lead to a room just under Mr. Ennis' apartment.*

I try the handle, but the door's locked. I reach up and feel heat coming through the slits in the doorway. *Laundry? No, the laundry room is on the other side of the building. Maybe it's the water heater. But then where did the cat go?*

I stand there for a minute, putting my ear to the door. I hear a clunking noise, the kind of thing I've been hearing now and then throughout the complex. *There it goes again. Guess I solved that one.*

I hear a low moaning sound, and I feel hot breath on my face, coming from the slits in the doorway. It's rancid, like rotting trash. I cover my nose and mouth, but I still find myself drawn to the source of it.

I put my ear back to the door. Then I hear something louder. An awful, guttural sound belches from behind the door. Nothing human could make that sound. I feel it shake me to my core, and I jump backwards, bumping my head hard on the underside of the steps.

"Ow!" I cry out, holding my head. I wince in pain, closing my eyes as I keep walking backwards. Once I'm in the courtyard I open my eyes and my vision spins as I stare upward. The sun is bearing down hard now. I'm dizzy. I can see the doorway in my mind. It's like it's floating above me, down a long, white hallway. I feel like I'm running toward it, then falling, falling as the hallway tips forward and I lose my step. It feels like I'm falling forever before I finally hit the ground.

CHAPTER 9

I guess it was Alfonso who found me and carried me back up to the apartment. I wake up to find him and Dad staring down at me.

"Rosie!" Dad says as I open my eyes.

"*Princesa,* you OK?" Alfonso asks.

"Ow …" I groan. "I hit my head."

"Don't worry, we'll take you to the doctor this afternoon. You have to go get your checkup before school starts anyway."

"I think it's better if you go now, no?" Alfonso says.

"Alfonso …" Dad begins, as if Alfonso has crossed some unmarked boundary. Then he looks at me, and I must look pretty miserable, because he says, "OK, we'll go now."

They help me up, but I'm so dizzy they need to hold onto me as I walk. A sharp pain shoots through my ankle. I cry out again.

"She hurt her ankle, too!" Alfonso says.

"I can see that," Dad says.

Alfonso helps Dad take me to the car and leaves.

Dad tells me he'll be right back and disappears for a few minutes. I'm clutching an ice pack and a towel to the back of my head when he runs back to the car holding the Yellow Pages.

"Dad, what are you doing?" I ask.

"Rosie, we need to find a doctor," he says.

"Oh." I can't think straight, but I still realize how odd he's being. *He's probably really freaked out and ashamed*, I think.

Dad drives me to a free clinic in nearby Glendale. The doctor ends up being OK, a youngish guy with a goatee who looks like he was in a band once. I end up needing two stiches in the back of my head, which I haven't even realized has been bleeding this whole time, ruining my favorite "Far Side" T-shirt. My ankle is a little sprained, but it's not so bad. They're nice enough to lend me some crutches, and the doctor tells me to take Tylenol and go easy for a bit.

I spend the next few days watching old movies in bed, one of my favorite pastimes with Mom. But I keep thinking about what happened. *It's weird that I twisted my ankle like that — I don't remember it happening. It's almost like ... something did it to me.*

But I've always had a weird pain there when I run a lot — hence the lack of sports in my life. *It's gonna be even worse now after falling on it several times, Rosie. Smooth move, klutz.*

Unfortunately, school is about to start. So, I'm going to start school with crutches and staples in my head. *Great!*

I'd been perfectly fine being lazy all summer, but suddenly I'm restless when there's nothing I can do about it. I feel like I missed my chance to do something with myself this summer. I could have tried harder to meet people and make friends, or asked Dad to enroll me in some sort of activity. All I've done is watch the latest season of "Real World" twice at Jimmy's, sketch a few pictures of the people in the apartment complex and the tree outside my window, and write down all the lyrics to my Smashing Pumpkins tape in a notebook.

Between the pain and restlessness, I start sleeping terribly, so I'm really tired in the days leading up to school. Dad's busy writing and trying to "network," which sounds more like begging over the phone for coffee dates, so he can't really deal with my whining.

Suddenly, it's the day before the first day of school. I had been hopeful, excited even. But now I just feel run down. I was hoping to have my stitches out and have lost the crutches by the first day of school, but no such luck. *How can I try to be more than what I am, when I feel like this?*

I hobble downstairs to buy myself a candy bar and cheer myself up. Dad is too wrapped up in himself to tend to me more than he already has, and I decide that I should try moving around anyway to practice for tomorrow. I get to the laundry room and — *yes!* — one last Whatchamacalit is in the vending machine.

I don't even wait — I start chowing down on it right then and there. I catch my reflection in the vending machine glass.

"Oof," I say, eyeing my stitched-up head and mouth full of chocolate. "You look rough, Rosie."

Still chewing, I get closer to examine a pimple. "You probably aren't helping," I say to the candy bar. My breath starts to fog up the glass. Before I can wipe it away, an image starts to appear, slowly at first. It's like an invisible finger is drawing on the machine. I stand there, mouth agape, watching as the numbers appear on their own: "301."

*

I roll around in bed. I hurried as quickly as I could manage back to the apartment and immediately got into bed. I told myself that it was nothing. Maybe someone wrote it there before and it was just left over.

But I know that's not true. *You saw numbers appear on their own. That isn't normal.*

"C'mon, big tree," I say to the sycamore, its shadows dancing across my room. I watch its limbs sway with the wind, which always calms me down. I fall asleep and wake up again, on and off, for a few hours.

I sense light dancing across my closed eyelids, then it turns off again like a switch. *Dad?*

I open my eyes and wipe away the crust. "Dad?" I ask weakly.

There's a faint silhouette sitting silently on the end of my bed. It looks like a man crouching down. But its head is misshapen. It's more of the suggestion of a person. Solid blue eyes stare down at me from an otherwise featureless void, and I'm sure that it's been watching me. It moves slightly, and I see that its legs are bent the wrong way.

I gasp and back up against the headboard. I want to scream, but I can't bring myself to make a sound as I stare at this being, shifting inhumanly and staring down at me. I squeeze my eyes shut so hard that I see stars. When I open them again, the little stars trickle around in my vision. I scan the room, breathing heavily as my eyes adjust to the dark, but whatever was there before has vanished.

Breathing heavily, I look around the room. I lift the bed skirt and look under the bed. All I see is a giant drawing pad Aunt Rita gave me after Mom died.

Dreading what I might find, I slide open the closet door and back away. Still, there's nothing to be seen other than clothing.

"Just a stupid dream," I say, trying to calm myself down. I toss myself back onto the bed and turn over onto my side.

But my heart is still racing. I lie there, staring at the door. *My door was closed. How could something have gotten in and out so quickly?* Regardless of how crazy it seems, I can still see that featureless, humanoid *thing* in my mind. I remember how it felt to wake up knowing that it had been looming over me. I toss and turn for the rest of the night; every time I start to fall asleep, I think about those ghostly blue eyes staring down at me.

CHAPTER 10

I'm wired. My heart feels like it's punching through my chest. I knew I'd be nervous on the first day, but it's worse than it would've been after whatever it was I saw last night. Still, I can't waste time thinking about whatever it is I think I saw. Seventh graders aren't supposed to see ghosts in the dark. That's kid stuff.

"Are you excited?" Dad asks, drumming his fingers on the steering wheel to R.E.M.'s "Losing My Religion."

"Yeah, I am," I say.

"Are you scared? It's OK to be scared."

"No." *Not of school, anyway.*

"Do you want me to come with you and make sure everything's OK?"

"No!" I say firmly. "I can figure it out, Dad. It's fine."

It's raining, which is weird for California, I guess. We pull up to the school. Its green and white archways beckon me in.

"Good luck, honey!" Dad says as I open the door. "Be careful on that ankle! Don't slip again!"

"Dad, shut up!" I call back.

I push myself on my crutches through the open front doors, past throngs of kids in baggy jeans, striped long-sleeved shirts and string jewelry they got on vacation. I stare at the lockers on either side of me as if they're foreign entities—my last school was an elementary school, but there are sixth graders at this school, so I'm a little behind the game.

I dodge getting knocked over by screaming boys still full of summer energy and follow signs to the cafeteria, where I'm supposed to pick up my schedule. There's some confusion because I'm new. They have me under the wrong letter because of the "O" in "O'Connell." As if I'm the first person to attend Valley Village Junior High School with an Irish last name.

Because of the delay, I'm still waiting on my schedule when the bell rings. The assistant principal, Mrs. Sailor, arrives in a brown power suit, beaming so hard that it looks like her lips might burst. She shakes my hand furiously, welcoming me and insisting that she walk me to first period.

"I hear you're from Chicago," she says in a thick, Midwest accent. "So am I!"

"I'm not from Chicago," I say. "Galena."

"Oh, gosh, Galena sure is beautiful."

"Are you going to say anything about me to the class?"

"I'll just let the teacher know that you're new and that it took us a minute to get you situated," she replies, beaming her 10,000-watt smile and winking awkwardly through her asymmetrical fringe.

When we get to class, she pulls the kind of crap I really hoped she wouldn't.

"Class, we have a new student," she says, never breaking that smile. "Her name is Rose O'Connell. Now, some of you I've known a long time, so I know you'll make her feel welcome here."

I stare at the clock as she says this, unable to meet the gaze of any of the gawking homeroom kids.

"What happened to your leg?" a dark-haired girl asks. A few people laugh.

"Emily!" Mrs. Sailor says with a tone of mild exasperation.

"It's OK," I say, trying to sound tough. "I … hit my head."

"So why is your leg hurt?" Emily says more quietly, sending a couple of her friends into fits.

"Well it's nice to meet you, Rose," interrupts Ms. Torres, a pleasant-looking thirtysomething woman with a square-shaped hairstyle.

"Rosie," I mutter.

"Excuse me?"

"Oh, call me Rosie."

"Rosie O'Connell?" Emily says. "That sounds like Rosie O'Donnell."

The class erupts in laughter. "Emily, that's quite enough out of you!" Mrs. Sailor says sternly. But it's too late. I slump to an empty chair and stare up at the clock. *Just five more hours and fifty-two minutes to go.*

CHAPTER 11

The first few days of school are pretty uneventful — at first. I haven't made any friends yet. I've tried a few times to talk to my new classmates, but the words seem to get stuck in my mouth.

I'm new, so my locker is by all the sixth graders, and I know making friends with them would be the equivalent of enlarging the already substantial target on my back. No one really talks to me, except to ask what happened to my leg, before quickly walking away.

The one exception is Señora Chang. She's Chinese, obviously, but she's also my Spanish teacher. In her lessons, she talks about alternative music, and she has a poster of this '80s band called The Cure on her wall, with the words "La Cura" printed above their towering hairsytles.

Mostly, it's just me by myself. The trick to not feeling alone, or *looking* like you're alone, is seeming like you have somewhere to go. So I hobble around the halls or spend my lunches sticking around to chat with Señora Chang about music. Or I wander through the halls to check my locker for the 14th time, before finally sitting down with my sad sandwich under a tree for 10 minutes. That's about the longest I can handle without feeling like a total loser.

Not that I'm dying to be friends with anyone in particular here. So far, no one can hold a candle to my friends back home. There *is* one person who seems interesting: Alex Riojas. He sits in front of me in Señora Chang's class. I don't really notice him at first; I don't think any of the girls do. Then, on the third day of school, he shows up with his hair bleached and spiked up like Thom Yorke, much to the "oohing" and "ahhing" of other kids in the class. Señora Chang decides to change his Spanish name from "Alejandro" to "Rubio" because of it.

But it's not the hair; it's that he doesn't seem to care what she or anyone else thinks, even the jocks who call him gay because of his hair or how skinny he is. *I wish I could be like that.* But all I've done so far to get his attention is ask to borrow a pen from him every time lecture is about to start, I haven't thought up the second part of that brilliant scheme yet.

At this point, "Hey, Rosie O'Donnell!" is about the most attention I get from the idiot seventh-grade boys. Apparently, word travels fast if you're a new kid with a stupid nickname. One day, as I'm putting away my U.S. history book, I overhear Emily, the pig-tailed, popular blonde girl who gave me this unfortunate nickname, which was probably her most original idea of the decade, talking about me with her friends.

"Where did she come from?" I hear Lauren, her inexplicably popular, horse-faced friend ask.

"I dunno, Illinois or something," Emily says. "I think she gets bussed in." I guess she's been paying attention.

"Ew," Mia says. Emily laughs. Mia is their tall, jock friend. As one of the only black girls at our school, she holds a certain *cool* factor that I'm sure isn't lost on Emily and Lauren, who are otherwise dull as rocks.

"Shh," Emily says. "I don't want anyone to tell on me," she says pointedly, without looking at me.

At this point, U.S. History goes sailing to the floor in a loud *THUMP*. All of the girls snicker. "Smooth move, Rosie O'Donnell!" Mia calls out as they walk off to the cafeteria.

"Cool," I say out loud to myself. *It's fine. I don't want to be friends with those girls. Mia is mean because she's too tall for boys to want to talk to her, Lauren is mean because she's horse-faced. Emily's just a boring cheerleader type who'll do whatever's expected of her all the time. They wouldn't want to be friends with me, either, if they knew how mean I was deep down. They don't want to be friends, anyway.*

After about a week, Dad finally asks, "How's school, honey? Do you love it yet?"

Lately, he's been out more often than not. I think he might have found a girlfriend because I heard him doing gross baby talk on the phone one night. He hasn't said anything about a girlfriend, much less brought her around yet. All I know is he's never called *me* his little "tootsie wootsie" before.

"Yeah, it's fine," I say. I realize it sounds insincere, but he doesn't notice.

"I knew you'd love it and fit in better here," he says.

Fit in better here. I thought I fit in just fine with my friends back home. Sara, Renée, Jessica ... I miss them. We weren't cool or anything; we still played with dolls and cared more about ponies and the boys on "Swans Crossing" and "Saved By the Bell" than real-life boys, but we didn't care. The rest of the world didn't really matter to us. Here ... no one is really anything like me.

"Back to School Night is coming up. I'm excited to meet the other parents. You're not the only one who needs to make friends!"

"It seems like you're doing just fine."

"Huh?"

I roll onto the couch. "You're meeting people just fine. I'm not meeting anyone."

"Honey, maybe you can meet some of Daddy's new friends too,

when the time is right."

"I can see you're really worried about how I'm doing," I reply. I'm tired of faking it.

"How can you say that? Huh? Everything I do is for you, sweetie." He sighs. "I can't expect you to understand yet. But there are certain things I need to do to be successful in this town. Certain people I need to meet …"

He goes on, but I'm not really listening. As usual, it's 99 percent about him, but he doesn't see it that way. He starts rummaging through his typed pages.

"I was thinking about trying out for a sport or something, once my ankle gets better," I say.

"Honey, you don't really like sports, I thought."

"Yeah, I don't. I just feel like I should do something." Dad doesn't respond. "I'm not really making any friends through my charm."

"Uh huh."

"I was thinking about joining the circus."

"Mmm hmm."

"I was always a pretty good juggler."

"Do they have a juggling team?" he asks, absent-mindedly.

"Never mind, Dad."

"Honey, I hear you, I just can't find anything I wrote today. It was in the typewriter. Did you see where those pages went …"

I leave as he's tornadoing through papers and flop down onto my bed. Dad has no idea what it's like for me. He's always been kind of a freak, but he was popular in school and back home. I saw the way some of my mom's friends would look at him sometimes. And now I'm pretty sure he just confirmed having a girlfriend.

What does he know about being an outsider?

I'm exhausted, so I crawl into bed early. I haven't been sleeping well since the night before school started. I've been trying not to think about the weirdness around the apartment building. With school underway, I don't have time for those childish things anymore. It was probably all my imagination. I can't make any sense of what happened, anyway.

I stare at the closet door. In the moment, what I saw felt so real. It seemed like ... someone, or something, I could not only touch, but feel in the room with me. *How could that be? It was probably just pre-first day jitters. I really need to sleep. I haven't been able to focus much on schoolwork, and the last thing I need is to be failing school on top of being a limping loser with no friends.*

*

I'm in a restless slumber, tossing and turning to the sound of trucks and police cars in the night.

Suddenly, everything goes silent.

It wakes me up as quickly as if someone were playing loud music. I open my eyes and stare up at the ceiling. I can hear something ... that low hum, like someone left a blank tape playing. I sit for a minute, thinking about what it could be. *I might as well get up and use the bathroom.*

I look myself over in the mirror, pulling my eyelids down to look at my bloodshot eyes. I look pale and sad, instead of cheery and full of life like Emily, but I'm a little taller and thinner than I was at the beginning of summer. I guess most girls would be happy about that. I start to poke at a zit, but some movement distracts me. *Is there something crawling in my hair?*

I momentarily forget my injury and slap my hand over my head. "Oww!" I say. Still wincing at the pain, I run my fingers through my hair, but there's nothing other than my new scar.

I'm focused on my reflection when I swear I see the shower curtain rustle behind me again. I gasp and turn around, but it's motionless. *It's probably all in your head, dummy. Maybe you shook something loose when you hit your head.*

Just then, I hear faint padding, *tap tap tap,* as if something's slinking around the apartment. I whip out of the bathroom and look into the hallway. I see nothing, of course. I'm not even sure if I saw or heard anything. It feels like the memory of someone or something that happened. *I'm losing it. I should get some rest,* I think. *But what if ... it's not nothing?*

From the hallway I scan up and down the walls of the family room. The window blinds are half-open, and light and shadows move across the carpet. *Is someone walking by?*

I peek between the blinds. It's dark out, save for the fluorescent lights blaring out of the fixtures. But I can't see anyone walking outside.

When I turn around, I see shadows dancing across the floor. They're shortening, gyrating, and they're moving toward the door to Dad's bedroom. I stare as the shadows writhe and seem to form a united whole. Then they slip underneath the door like smoke, without a sound.

OK, I couldn't have imagined that. I have to help Dad!

But I'm too terrified to open the door. I get down on my hands and knees and peer underneath. I can't see anything. But I can feel a frigid cold that pierces through the late summer night. Dread ties my stomach in knots. I feel the phantom of something caressing my neck and I stand up quickly. Vapor comes out of my mouth in small clouds as my breath comes out in heaves.

Then, as suddenly as it happened, there's nothing. The low hum vanishes. The air feels still again and warm again, and the feeling that I'm not alone has all but vanished.

I put my face into my hands and breathe deeply. *Jeez, Rosie. Just go back to sleep.*

I stand and walk back into the other room. I'm going to close the blinds when I see a figure move across the window. I topple backwards a few steps and see the outline of wiry gray hair.

It's him! Mr. Ennis!

The figure stops and turns, and stares into the window. I'm on the floor at this point, staring up at it. *Oh God, he's going to see me!*

The figure gets closer to the window. It sees me At this point, there's nothing I can do. It raises a hand at me.

I get a better look, and it's Mrs. Lieberman, holding Coco or Peanut. She sees me and waves slowly, a smile plastered across her face. I stare at her bewildered, and she lifts the cat's paw to wave at me along with her. Without knowing what else to do, I wave back, still breathing heavily on the floor.

Mrs. Lieberman suddenly turns and walks back toward her apartment. I get myself up, limp back to bed and pull the duvet over my head.

*

Thinking back to these events the next morning, I can't figure out when I was asleep or awake — or if I was awake at all. Whatever I thought I saw last night, it could've easily been a dream, and chances are that it was. *I was probably just freaked out because of old Mrs. Lieberman walking around the apartment building in the middle of the night. I need to get it together.*

I thought I got over my fear of the dark when I was a little girl. I'd call out to Mom, and she'd come in and turn on a nightlight for me when she was still healthy. But I left that nightlight behind when we moved, and seventh graders don't have nightlights. I can't ask for one.

CHAPTER 12

Dad's out again. I'm at Jimmy and Vera's for the afternoon.

"Let's play tag," Jimmy says as I'm tunneling my hand through a bag of Lay's.

"Jimmy, I can't play tag anymore."

"Why not?"

I tap my foot with my hand, which is covered in chip dust. I've been off the crutches, but after agitating it during Halloween, I'm not running around any time soon.

"What about 'adventure'?"

"Jimmy," I say, sighing. I get embarrassed if anyone older walks by while we're playing an imaginary game. "I think we're getting too old for that."

"Oh," he says, disappointed.

Even though I don't feel like doing much of anything, I decide it's better to do something than send Jimmy off into a difficult mood. "Why don't we go wandering around the construction site?"

"Hell yeah!" he says.

I get permission from Vera, telling her we're just going to go buy gum and Cokes at the nearby 7-11, and we leave to go snooping around the construction site adjacent to the apartment complex. They're building some sort of mini-mall, which would be nice to have, but for now it's just a hollow frame and a big dirt pit. It's not much to see, but it feels kind of fun and dangerous to go there, even though it's not so far from the apartment that we can get in any real trouble. Strangely, no one's been working on it since the summer. We hop into the skeletons of future buildings, giggling as we try to scare each other by jumping out from behind the larger beams.

"I bet this is gonna be a J.C. Penny," I tell him. But Jimmy has lost interest in our conversation and is poking around in the mud with a stick.

"Jimmy …" I don't know how to ask what I'm going to ask without sounding crazy, but he's not judgmental, and I don't know who else to talk to. "Do you ever … see stuff? Like in the apartment building?"

Jimmy keeps poking around for a second, then stops suddenly. "What stuff?"

"Uh, like, weird things."

"Some people are weird."

"Yeah, some people are weird. Like the guy on the second floor, right? Mr. Ennis."

Jimmy looks at me wild-eyed.

"Uh, that's not really what I'm talking about, though. Like, something moving around, but when you check, there's nothing there."

"Well, if there's nothing there, then why do you think there is? Something must be there."

I find Jimmy's logic oddly comforting. "Yeah, maybe. I dunno, I feel like I'm going crazy."

"You shouldn't say that," he says firmly.

"Sorry," I say. I haven't thought about what a hard time Jimmy must have in school. We don't have the same schedule because of his special needs, so I almost never see him.

"It's more like … you remember something that happened so much that it's like it's happening to you right then and there."

"Let's go home!" Jimmy says suddenly, ignoring me and racing off toward the muddy ditch that extends between the site and the apartment building. Only he doesn't stop in time.

"Jimmy!" I cry out, hurrying after him. I try my best not to trip over the uneven areas of the site—now that I'm off the crutches and my stitches are out, I'm in no rush to mess myself up again. By the time I reach the ditch, Jimmy's already tumbled into the mud.

I climb down carefully after him, taking care not to get my new Skechers too dirty. I find Jimmy at the bottom of the ditch, lying in a dirt heap, crying.

I give him a second. "Jimmy … come on," I say, extending my hand. He stops crying and stares down at the mud. I don't know what to make of him at this point. He's staring at a fixed point, but it doesn't look like there's anything there.

"Sometimes," he says, "I do see things that aren't there. Then the other kids think I'm weird."

He sits staring at that same spot in the mud. I look up at the sky and give him another minute.

"Hey, don't listen to them," I finally say. "I don't think you're weird. If you're weird, I'm weird."

I want to ask him what he means, but I'm afraid I scared him, and I don't want him to start crying again. Anyway, maybe I don't really want to know what he means. It's getting dark, and I want to get out of the mud and go back inside.

"C'mon, Jimmy," I say. I help him up, and we trudge back to the apartment. He's tracking mud everywhere and sulking.

"What on Earth did you two get up to? Rosie, I need you to be better with him," Vera says as we enter the apartment. She towels off Jimmy's face. I'm hurt by her words, but I can tell she's just startled. I clean myself off, and Jimmy showers while I scan basic cable for something good. "Poltergeist" is on; normally I'd make Jimmy watch it with me, but I'm not really in the mood for that right now.

Jimmy comes out of his room dressed in striped sweats and starts playing with a toy racecar. *We're too old for that, too, Jimmy*, I think. But I don't point that out. And I realize he's not really playing with it, per se. He just glides it along the same spot of carpet over and over again, watching the wheels spin. It must be comforting to him. I'm just glad he hasn't gone completely anti-social tonight. I don't have any other friends, and I don't feel like being alone at the moment. I pull Karen out of my bookbag and set her down next to us. Jimmy crashes his car into her, and we both laugh.

"Do you wanna watch TV?" I ask him. I flip on the TV, and a "Fresh Prince" rerun is on. Jimmy ignores me, as he often does, and keeps racing his car along the carpet. I gather Karen and move to the couch.

"Hey, do you guys want to order pizza?" Vera asks from the kitchen.

"Pizza!" Jimmy replies emphatically.

"I was trying to make a stew, but it's not very good," Vera says as I walk into the kitchen. Her blonde hair is growing out, and she's tied it up with a red handkerchief. She's wearing a faded sundress that has to be 10 years old or from a thrift store. I think about how great she looks without even trying and how cool she must have been when she was my age.

"It smells good," I offer.

"I'll just eat it later myself. Healthy shit," she says, smirking at me. I look down, a little embarrassed. "It's OK," she says. "About Jimmy. It's not your fault."

"I know. I mean, I'm sorry anyway," I reply.

"It's just hard sometimes," she says, stirring the pot. "I'm really grateful to have you around, you know. You're great with him."

"Oh, it's no problem," I say. Now I feel extremely embarrassed, for Jimmy and for myself. "I mean, I don't really have anywhere else to go … and I like it here."

"That's good that you do," she says, putting down the ladle. "To hell with this thing. I'm calling Domino's."

I walk back to the TV and scan the channels. Jimmy's tinkering with his car, lying on the carpet like a cat and holding it into the air, flicking the wheels with his fingers. The pizza arrives, and the three of us sit munching and watching the news. It's pretty boring. I heard Vera and Dad chatting about Kuwait once, and I want to pay attention so I can participate next time, but I feel helpless to my eyes closing. I go outside to see if Dad's back yet, but the lights are still off in our apartment.

"You're always welcome to stay here, lovey," Vera offers, even pulling sheets out of the cupboard.

"No, I should really go home. Dad'll be back," I say.

Vera sets the sheets down on the couch. "Well, you're welcome, just the same."

Part of me wants to stay, but I can't believe Dad would be so careless to stay out so late without saying anything. Even for him, it's pretty bad. But also, I don't know what kind of night I'm going to have, and I don't want to put Jimmy and Vera through whatever crap I'm going through.

Vera's in and out of the room, folding laundry and tidying up, while Jimmy has passed out in front of the TV, on top of his race-car. I doze on and off. Vera finally takes Jimmy to his room and makes a bed for me on the couch. "Feel free to lie down, lovey, and I'll wake you up when your Dad comes back."

"Thanks," I say. "Can I stay up for him and watch TV?"

"Of course."

Vera shuts off the lights and goes to bed. I finish watching "Dead at 21," and Kurt Loder and the "MTV News" globe spin before my closing eyes.

*

I jolt awake. The clock on the VCR blinks 12:00 a.m. *The power must've gone out. What time is it?*

I could have sworn I heard something.

Then I hear it again through an open window. Keys jingling. *Dad must finally be back.*

I grab Karen from off my lap and open the door, looking to either side. There's nothing to my left, toward our apartment. Then I look to my right.

I see another set of keys dangling again in the door of apartment 301. I rub my eyes to make sure I'm not seeing things. *It's impossible someone would be in there at this hour. Maybe Mr. N left them in the door again? But then why would they be swaying?* It's dead calm outside. The grimy walls of the apartment complex shield us from any outside breeze.

I don't know what moves me forward. Suddenly, I'm at the door of apartment 301, staring at the doorknob.

I reach down and turn the knob. It opens without me even having to unlock the door.

Inside, it's the same as before: it looks like our apartment, but slightly different. It's odd to be in a place that's almost the same as your own, but with enough points of difference to feel alien. Everything looks either smaller or bigger when there's nothing and no one inside.

My feet make barely any sound on the carpet, seeming to sink in with each awkward step. My feet wobble, as if I'm walking in reverse.

In the kitchen, it looks like whatever was there on the floor before has been cleaned up. When I look up, I see a faint light coming from the bedroom door at the end of the hallway. *Maybe Mr. N left the light on.*

Before I can decide whether or not to walk down the hall, the door to the room opens. It's dark, except for the same faint source of light.

My eyes focus on the light. I can see now that the light outlines a dark figure that is slowly moving toward me.

I stare, unmoving. My feet feel plastered to the floor.

The light gets slightly brighter as it moves closer to me. I can see it in better definition now. The outline of hair. Or what would be hair on a person. It's long, like a woman's hair. But the figure is about my height. The figure glides forward with no other movement. Her movement feels graceful, but unnatural.

Then it dawns on me: I recognize her. The girl I saw in my room, the one from the dream I had on the journey to L.A., and the one standing in front of me now … they're one and the same. She's here, in this apartment.

My feet finally disconnect from the floor and I back up into a cupboard door. I feel stuck again. I can't tell if anything is holding me there, other than fear. Suddenly, the air feels thick, like a warm blanket.

The figure stops moving. We both stand motionless, staring at one another. My mouth is agape in wonder as I stare at her soft, glowing frame. I try to speak, but nothing comes out.

We stand there a moment in silence. I try to study her features, but every time I feel like I can make something out, the definition of her face seems to vanish. All I can see are her black, hollow eyes that stare at me quizzically. As if she's doing the same thing to me.

I can't take the silence anymore. Weakly, I finally say, "Hi." I can't think of what else to possibly say to a ghost, or a shadow, or … whatever this is.

To my surprise, she answers.

"Hello," she says, her voice high and whispery, sounding like several voices intertwined.

I gasp. *What do I do? This is unreal!*

"You … visited me before, didn't you?"

"Yes," she says.

"Who are you?"

"… I'm a girl, just like you."

I laugh a little. "You're … just like me?"

"Yes," she says, giggling a little, too.

Silence again. "Why are you here?" I finally ask. She stares at me intently, almost sadly.

Before either of us can speak again, I'm tumbling backwards, out the doorway. I'm floating quickly, my arms and legs flailing in the night air. I feel myself lie back down on the couch in Jimmy and Vera's apartment. My head hits the pillow, and all I see is darkness and the small glowing light of the VCR clock. It's not flashing anymore — the digits 12:13 glow, unblinking.

I hear another jingling.

I yawn and sit up, shaking off the feeling of waking up from a realistic dream, only in this case, it's not unwelcome. I trudge toward the front door and open it. I look to my right and see nothing out of the ordinary.

Looking to my left, I see the door to our apartment closing. I go back and quickly put my shoes on, stuff Karen back into my backpack and leave Vera and Jimmy's apartment as quietly as possible.

Dad's keys are still in the door. I peer in and see him stumbling around, murmuring to himself as he pours a glass of water. "Down you go, Danny boy," he says, the water dribbling out of the sides of his mouth. He starts coughing violently, and I hide against the wall instinctively. I can't face him like this.

I wait, staring out into the dark courtyard with the door to our apartment cracked open, until I hear him flush the toilet and drag himself to bed. Finally, I take the keys out of the door, enter the apartment, close the door softly and place the keys on the kitchen counter. I crawl into bed as quietly as possible.

But once I'm in bed, I can't sleep. I was so tired before that I could hardly stay awake. Now I'm confused. The confusion gradually gives way to anger. *How could he stay out like that without saying anything? Or even check on me once he got in? And did he drive drunk?* I lie like that for 45 minutes or an hour but finally calm down by telling myself I'll have a good reason for my foul mood in the morning. *Plus,* I think, seeing my mud-streaked old Levi's in the corner, *I could use some new clothes.*

CHAPTER 13

I expect for Dad to brush everything off like he usually does. "Oh Rosie, you're such a worry wart, you could've just stayed at Jimmy's," he'll probably say. But to my surprise, he's apologetic.

"Honey," he says, gripping my shoulder from behind as I polish off some Frosted Mini Wheats. "I'm so sorry I stayed out without calling. Were you OK?"

"Yeah, Dad, I was fine," I say, masking my surprise. "I was at Jimmy's. Where were you?"

"Oh, honey. I got caught up with some new friends. But that's no excuse. I'm so, so sorry. Can you ever forgive me?"

He sounds pathetic, not at all like a parent should. But then he's never really acted like a parent. I'm embarrassed for him.

"Yeah, it's OK," I assure him. I'm annoyed because he's managed to diffuse my right to be in a bad mood.

"What can I do to make it up to you?"

I start to think about the clothes I wanted. Now, that thought seems so far away. "You could take me home," I say, flatly.

"What if I brought some of it here to you?" he says.

I have to hand it to Dad — he always knows how to surprise me. "What do you mean?"

"Why don't you ask one of your friends to come visit us over the winter break? It's on me."

"Really? Are you serious?"

"Yes. We can't leave to go back home so soon, but your dad's been doing really well," he says. I don't know what he means by that, but in the moment I don't care. "We can afford to bring one of your little friends here to visit. What was her name — Jennifer?"

"Jessica," I say. "Oh my God, thanks, Dad! I'll call her right now."

Jessica is my best friend from back home. We were part of an inseparable foursome that did everything together, but she was really there for me when Mom died. I was so sad, crying one minute, staring at the wall the next. Jessica stayed with me through all of it. So of course I want to see her. I feel like I owe her, too.

"Duh, of course," Jessica says on the phone when I ask her to come, as if it were completely up to her. But I know Jessica's parents are a lot cooler than most. Despite holding her to very high academic standards, they let her swear and stay up late, just as long as she gets good grades. Once she got a C in science, and I wasn't allowed to talk to her for a month, even at school. She calls me back in five minutes and tells me that her parents have agreed to let her come — she must have kept her grades up, then.

The next few weeks drag on, but soon enough, it'll be Christmas break. I haven't really made any friends at school or done anything with myself to speak of. I'm sort of at a loss when it comes to making friends here, so I stop trying.

Jessica's upcoming visit is all that keeps me going. Days turn into long bouts of struggling to pay attention. But, almost subconsciously, I start thinking again about the things I've seen. *What was all that?* I don't want to dream about them again; my sleep is finally improving. But I can't get them out of my head.

One day, in Spanish class, Señora Chang is going on about *el sub-*

juntivo and I really can't focus. I start trying to remember what the figures in my dreams looked like and sketching them out in my notebook. The girl I saw. Her glowing hair. Why can't I remember anything else about how she looked? And that thing I saw at the end of my bed. Those piercing blue eyes. Those legs that bent backwards ...

"What are you drawing?" It's Lauren, Emily's dumb lackey who sits in front of me in Spanish. It's more of an accusation than a question. She's hoping to discover something more to torment me with. Lauren's not as quick as Emily, though. She can't touch me.

I quickly shut my notebook. "None of your business," I say coldly. I startle Lauren, and even myself. I usually just try and shake off their teasing, but this is different — as if calling this thing back to mind causes me to be someone else. Another version of me I never dare show anyone.

"Whatever," she says, her auburn hair whipping me in the face as she turns around. "So weird ..." I hear her mutter.

"What did you say?" I ask, leaning in.

"Rosita," Señora Chang says.

"Lo siento," I say quietly, leaning back into my chair. Now I feel terrible. If there's anyone I don't want to let down, it's Señora Chang, but I'm sick of those girls being rude to me for no reason. There's nothing I can do, I guess. I crumple the drawing quietly and go back to writing out *quiera, quieras, quieramos ...*

As class ends, Señora Chang asks me to stay a minute, which draws the usual dumb seventh-grade "oohs." I'm filled with dread. *How could I have disappointed her like that?*

"Rosita ... Rosie, you know, just 'cause I think you're really cool, I can't give you special treatment."

I'm relieved. "I'm so sorry, Señora Chang. It won't happen again."

She shrugs. "It's fine. Are those girls bothering you? Lauren and Emily?"

I look down. "No, they're dumb, but it's fine."

"Ay, Rosie," she says. "You know what? I had girls like that in my school too, growing up."

"Yeah, but I'm not cool like you."

"Cool?" Señora Chang walks to her desk, then rummages through her purse for a minute. She pulls a Polaroid out of her wallet and shows it to me.

In it, I can see an Asian girl about my age with a poofy perm and overalls. She's wearing so much blush and eyeshadow that it looks like she got into a fight.

"Oh gosh! Were you friends with that girl?"

"Rosie," she says. "That's me. In the seventh grade. The popular girls had started wearing makeup, so I begged, *begged* my parents to let me wear makeup. I told them that American students are judged by their appearance and that girls who don't wear makeup get their grades docked."

"Are you serious? That's pretty genius, actually."

"Yeah, except then my mom overdid it to make sure I got *really* good grades and made me look like the clown from *It*."

I cover my mouth, cracking up. I can't help it. "I'm sorry."

"It's not funny! Well … it is funny. But I got made fun of for the entirety of seventh grade. You know my first name is Betty, right?"

I didn't know that. She must have told me, or told the class at some point. I can be pretty self-absorbed, Dad sometimes tells me.

"Rosie?" she says.

"Sorry, yeah, I remember you told us before."

"Anyway, the popular girls called me 'Bozo Betty' the entire year."

"Oh my gosh! You've got to be kidding me."

"I'm not kidding. But I got over it. I got into punk rock, did my own thing and found my people. You'll find yours, too. Just keep being your awesome self and hold on a little longer."

I sigh. "Thanks, Señora Chang."

"Don't worry about it. And don't tell anyone about Bozo Betty, or I'll fail you!"

Later that day, I think about what Señora Chang said. She made me feel a lot better, but it still bothers me, thinking about those girls. I lay on my couch, listening to the Gin Blossoms, my mind swimming. *What's their deal, anyway? What will I do after Jessica leaves? It's not like school is just gonna go away. I need to focus on the day-to-day. Maybe Señora Chang's right. I should try making some friends.*

Oh well, that's in the future, I think, flipping the tape. *Nothing I have to worry about now that Jessica's almost here.*

CHAPTER 14

"Wow, cool apartment," Jessica offers upon entering.

"You like it?" Dad asks.

"Yeah, it's so different than back home!" she says. Her brown eyes are miles wide and her dark bob bounces when she speaks. She told me her mom let her cut her hair like Uma Thurman in *Pulp Fiction*, but I think it looks more like Natalie Portman's. Either way, she looks so much older than the last time I saw her. I run my finger through my frizzy locks and wonder if I could even try looking like that.

Jessica's always been so good with adults. In the car, she told me and Dad everything that had been going on since we left, answering Dad's questions easily. I wish I could do things as casually as she does. She also knows exactly how to handle Dad — something I've never quite mastered.

"Thanks! It's a lot cozier, but we're pretty happy here," Dad said, winking at me. Weird. He doesn't wink. It's almost to say, *I know you aren't happy yet, but you will be.* I roll my eyes.

Dad lets us have the living room and goes to his room to try to write, coming out every so often to check on us and offer us more soda and snacks. I have to admit, it's really nice having Jessica around. Dad hasn't been around this much in a long time. It almost feels normal, me and a friend hanging out while Dad acts like a real parent for a change. I almost feel happy.

"You remember David?" Jessica asks.

"David … Collins?" I ask.

"No, he moved away," she says. "David Rector was in our class in the second grade, then he left and came back in fifth grade but he was in another class."

"Oh, kind of," I say. Jessica is so good with people. I get lost in my own world a lot of the time.

"He got really tall. All the girls like him now. He sits right by me in English and we talk every day. So now Jenna and Molly and all those girls ask me about him all the time. It's like I'm some weird celebrity to them."

I laugh. I haven't thought about any of these people in what feels like forever. The popular girls. Jessica almost sounds like she's friends with them now. I've never heard her talk about boys before.

"What's it like here?"

"Oh, it's OK," I say, unsure if Dad is listening. I sigh. "It kinda sucks, actually. I miss you guys."

"Yeah, we miss you too. What kind of music do you like?"

"Oh, my favorite band is Stone Temple Pilots. Look at all the tapes I got this summer." I take her to my growing collection. "I made you this mixtape last weekend when I was bored. Here."

"Oh cool, thanks," she says.

"So what bands do you like?"

"Oh, David made me all these awesome punk tapes. Have you ever heard Misspent Youth?"

"No. Do they have a video out?"

Jessica laughs "No, MTV sucks so bad. They wouldn't be on there."

I feel strangely offended. I felt like I was going to have all this knowledge and cool California experiences to share with Jessica when she came to visit. Suddenly I feel like I've been left behind.

"I know, it sucks," I say. "'The Real World' is fun to make fun of, though."

"Oh my God, it's so stupid."

"Should we watch it?"

"You guys have cable?"

"Yeah, Dad got it for us since he made us move here."

"Why'd you guys move, anyway?"

"Uh, my Dad said it was to give us a fresh start. I think it was more because he wanted to be in Hollywood."

This is the funniest thing Jessica has ever heard. "Are you serious? That's like the biggest joke. Does he want to be an actor?" she asks, lowering her voice.

"No, he's, like, writing stuff all the time and going out to meetings and stupid crap like that," I say.

Jessica tries to stifle her laughter. "Wait, have you read any of it yet?"

"No, he won't let me."

"Oh my God, we have to read it!"

"Shh, Jessica, he'll hear you."

I lead Jessica to the kitchen counter, where Dad has left a stack of papers.

"C'mon," she says. "I dare you."

I pick up the front sheet and we scan it together.

FADE IN:

EXT. SMOKE FILLED ALLEY – NIGHT

CUT TO:

A man pulls drives up in an old Lincoln town car. But it's not old, because this is the past. There's already another car waiting for him with its headlights on, spilling light into the night like milk on a dirty floor. The man exits the car and sees a tragically beautiful woman standing in the alley next to her car, holding an envelope.

                    WOMAN
          I thought you'd never show, Danny boy.

                    DANNY
     I haven't heard that name in years. How've you been, doll?

                    WOMAN
     Can't complain. But it looks like you're in a heap of trouble.

The woman hands Danny the envelope.

                    DANNY
          Is this why you brought me here in the dead of night?

                    WOMAN
     Take a look. I think you'll find these to be ... quite interesting.

Danny opens the envelope and takes out what appear to be crime scene photos. A woman lies in bed, apparently dead. In another photo, the same woman lies in the same spot, a pile of pills surrounding her.

                    DANNY
          You're saying there's foul play?

                    WOMAN
          You're the detective here.

Just then, a black town car pulls around the bend. Danny grabs the woman and pulls her around the corner. They crouch down as the car drives along. They peer through the windows and see a balding, middle-aged man sitting in the backseat. A stern-looking man in sunglasses drives the car.

> WOMAN
> That's Mayor O'Connell!

> DANNY
> You're right about that, doll. Ain't this funny?

> WOMAN
> Ain't what funny?

> DANNY
> (donning shades)
> The two of us here, just like old times. Just like shadows in the night …

Jessica and I are nearly crying with laughter.

"Oh my God, he put himself in the movie!" I say.

"Why is he putting on sunglasses if it's nighttime?" Jessica asks.

"Quick, put it back!" I say.

Jessica puts the page back down on top of the stack and we run over to the couch just as Dad comes in from the other room.

"It's so good to hear you laugh, honey," he says. This sends us into a fit. But I can't help but feel bad and catch him glance at me. Did he hear us? No, that's impossible.

We gorge on popcorn and watch MTV all night. The next day, Dad takes us to the mall. He lets us see "Dumb and Dumber," which puts us in a ridiculous mood all day. We can't stop laughing at all the weirdos walking around the North Hollywood Mall — the grunge guys in baggy jeans trying to rebel while drinking Orange Julius, the lame mall girls with nothing better to do than give these losers the time of day.

We're trying on ugly outfits at Nordstrom and making each other laugh while Dad wanders around the mall. I spy Lauren from school looking at bras with her mom. Even though we don't like each other, I'd normally say hey or something, but this would be too embarrassing for either of us because of … well, the bras. I whisper to Jessica, "There's this girl from my school. She's so rude. She and her friend made fun of me for being from Illinois."

"Ew, what a slut," she says, a little loudly. We hide behind a rack of undershirts before Lauren can see us.

"These are nice," I hear someone say. It must be Lauren's mom. "They look like they're in your size."

"Slut-size," Jessica says to me. We try to stifle our laughter.

"Mom, girls aren't wearing those anymore!" Lauren says in a whiney voice. This is too much for us. Jessica starts cackling and I join in. I see Lauren's long face peer around the aisle and shoot daggers at us as we scurry away.

"Rosie! I'm gonna remember that," I hear her say.

"Mummy, girls don't wear those anymore!" Jessica calls back in a faux bratty voice. It's perfect. I wish Jessica lived here all the time.

Later that week, we're in my room, not really doing anything. It's raining outside and there's nothing good on TV. I'm lying on my bed, staring at the ceiling, and Jessica is looking at random things in my room.

"Is this a troll doll?" she says, taking Karen off my bookshelf. *She knows full well what it is.* We were obsessed with our dolls in the fourth grade.

"Yeah, I still have her," I say. "She reminds me … of home, and

Mom."

"Oh," she says, realizing she's broached a touchy subject. "So, what are the guys like at 'Valley Village Middle School'?" she asks, emphasizing each word, as if I've put on airs.

"Shut up," I say. "I dunno, they're all dumb."

"Oh. That sucks."

"There's one guy I talk to, Jimmy."

"Oh really? What's he like?"

"Um, he's really quiet, but he's nice. He's a good listener."

"Is he cute?"

"No," I say, laughing, as if that's a preposterous question.

"We should call him."

"No! We can't." I've been dreading running into Jimmy the whole time Jessica was here. I'm just … not sure she'll understand.

"Why not?"

"I don't have his number."

"Can we look it up? I'm bored. I'll talk to him."

"No!" I say. "Don't call him."

"Fine."

We spend the rest of the night watching a Jonathan Taylor Thomas movie on TV in near silence. We finally talk later in my room. Jessica is lying on a pile of blankets and cushions on the floor.

"Ugh, that movie was so bad," she says.

"I know," I say. "Remember how much we used to like him?"

"*You* liked him," she says. "So, do you think you guys are gonna stay here?"

"I don't know. I hope not. I wanna go back."

"I dunno, it's pretty cool to be in California. It's so warm here."

"Yeah, but the people are lame," I say.

I sense Jessica growing tired of my negativity. I suddenly feel nervous about losing her as a friend forever.

My mind scans back to the past few months. The creature at the end of my bed. Being in apartment 301 and talking with the Shadow Girl in the middle of the night. I haven't thought about any of it that much since Jessica's been here. As if that reality can't exist at the same time as this one.

"Can I tell you a secret?" I ask, finally.

"Sure."

"I think this place is haunted."

"Really?"

"Yeah."

"How so?"

"Sometimes I see really weird things. The other night I swear I saw someone crouching at the end of my bed."

Jessica's jaw drops. "Are you serious? Are you OK?"

"Yeah, I'm fine."

"That's so weird. What was it?"

"It was nothing," I say. "I dunno. It's really hard to explain."

"Have you seen anything else?"

I think about *her*. "No. That was it."

I stop talking. A fart slips out.

Jessica and I start laughing hysterically. "Shh, we're gonna wake up my dad."

"I know, sorry. No offense, but your dad is so weird sometimes."

"Hey," I say, stiffening. I know she's right, but I still feel a little offended. "I mean, I guess so."

"You know my mom almost didn't let me come, right?"

I sit up. "Really?"

"Yeah. I think she was worried about it just being me, you and your dad."

That feeling of offense starts to turn into anger. "Why? What's her problem with Dad?"

Jessica sighs. "It's nothing."

"No, tell me."

"I guess," she starts. "Well, they all used to be friends, remember? Then … I dunno what happened. Maybe my mom just doesn't know him that well. She was closer with your mom."

"Yeah," I say. "Mom was really good about keeping up with friends. My dad is … kind of in his own world all the time."

"Hmm, that sounds familiar," Jessica asks, nudging me.

"Ugh, I'm nothing like him," I say and roll onto my side. "OK, good night."

"Good night," she says. We take her to the airport the next morning. As we drive away from the airport, I wonder if I'll ever see Jessica again.

CHAPTER 15

The happiness I felt during Jessica's visit comes crashing down over the next couple of days.

Back in Galena, it was really easy to have friends. Only a handful of people ever moved there or left — Karen's family is about the only one that I can remember moving away. I don't really even remember meeting Jessica or the others. Our families all knew each other already. It was almost predestined that we would end up being friends.

I'm sitting in Señora Chang's class for lunch, for the third time in a week. It started out just to help her clean up after a messy Taco Fiesta Friday, but now I keep finding excuses to hang out with her. It beats eating alone.

"I'm not bugging you, am I?" I ask her as I help erase the white-board.

"Of course not, Rosita," she says. She flips on KROQ, which is our favorite station. It's "Flashback Lunch," and I hear a woman's plaintive voice over some acoustic guitar as she sings "My name is Luka … I live on the second floor."

"Ugh," I say. "This song sounds so *old*."

"This is a great song!" she says.

"I guess," I say. "I like the vibraphone."

"You have a good ear. Why don't you join band?"

"I just know it because my Mom liked jazz," she says. "No

offense, Señora Chang, but band isn't exactly cool. I'm … having enough trouble already meeting people."

"Ay, Rosita," she says. "Well, who cares what anyone else thinks? At least you'd make some friends."

"I also can't really play anything," I say. I already thought about trying, but I don't want to be bad at something I'm not very interested in to begin with. If there's anything worse than being uncool, it's being uncool in the band. At least at the moment, I'm mostly invisible.

"Well, I'm running yearbook club now. We help put together the yearbook, pick photos, get quotes, lots of fun stuff. It starts later this year, so think about signing up."

"I'm not sure that's for me," I say.

"Why not? I think you'd be great for it. You don't want to just hang around here all the time, do you?"

"No," I say. I actually am fine with hanging out with Señora Chang all lunch as she's the only one who really gets me, but it sounds like the feeling isn't mutual. "I'm kind of hungry. I think I'm gonna take off."

"Oh come on, Rosita, I didn't mean anything by that. You're always welcome here."

"Thanks," I say. "But I'm OK."

I grab my ratty green Walmart backpack and hustle out the door. With that, I'm banished back to the bathrooms for the remainder of lunch. *Nice going, Rosie. Your only new friend in school is a teacher, and you even botched that.*

That night, I try talking to Dad, but he's not in the mood to chat, hurrying around the apartment and getting ready for a night out. He's wearing a tie, something I've never seen him do, except at weddings (and Mom's funeral). "There are SpaghettiOs and ramen in the pantry," he tells me.

"Jimmy's … not in the mood to talk," I say, having been by earlier.

"I think you're old enough now to handle a night on your own," he says, straightening his tie in the mirror. With that, he heads out the door.

Once he leaves, I'm rummaging around the kitchen and see a bunch of crumpled pages in the trash. I decide to pull them out, and to my horror, they're the pages Jessica and I were reading and laughing at. *Oh God, he must have heard us making fun of it. No wonder he's acting all hurt.*

I try watching TV, but I feel guilty and unsettled. I walk into the bathroom and stare at myself in the mirror, wondering what's wrong with me. Jimmy won't talk to me. I just pushed away Señora Chang, one of the only people that saw anything worthwhile in me. Not even my own dad feels like being around me.

I decide to go for a walk around the complex. I can't stand to watch TV right now. I can't stand to stay inside. I can't stand to be around me, either. I need to clear my head.

It's about 11 at night. No one's outside in the apartment complex. Just me and the fluorescent lights casting orange ovals on the walkways. If I squint, they look like eyes, staring back at me.

I walk by apartment 301 and stop. Something — or someone — clearly wants me here, and I can't ignore it any longer. I suddenly realize something — I never gave Mr. N the key back to the apartment, the one I pulled out of the door before right before I hit my head.

I run back to the apartment and go rummaging through my room, searching through my desk drawers. It's not there. I stare up at Karen on my shelf. As if she telepathically revealed it to me, I realize where it must be. I find the pair of bloodstained

Levi's I was wearing that day sitting on my closet floor —
they're ruined, but I love those jeans and couldn't bring myself
to throw them away. Sure enough, the key sits inside the front
pocket.

Before I walk out, I look back up at Karen. "Thanks, Karen," I say.
Her pearly blue eyes stare back, unchanging. I grab her off the
shelf and stuff her into my pocket — for protection.

Back outside apartment 301, my breathing quickens. *This is
what you wanted, right?* I unlock the door, walk inside and look
around. It's pretty dark. I don't know what I'm looking for. Then
it's like the thoughts start knocking down some door in my
brain. Somehow, I just know. I sit down in the dining area, on the
carpet where a little light shines in at the window. Cross-legged,
I close my eyes, as if meditating.

I open my eyes. Not all the way. I squint so I have a blurry view of
the hallway.

What are you doing, Rosie? What do you think is gonna happen?

I wait and I wait. But nothing happens.

I curl up on the floor, holding my knees to my body. I want to cry.
I miss Mom so much. I don't have anyone here. I close my eyes
and wish things were different.

After a while, I sit up, groggily. I must have dozed off for a bit.
OK, Rosie, it's time to get a grip, I think, rubbing my eyes.

When I focus my eyes, the shadow girl is standing just a few feet
away from me.

No part of her moves except her hair, each strand seeming to
possess its own mind, like the arms of an octopus.

As she approaches, I stand up, slowly. We stand there for a
minute, face to face. I can feel faint warmth emanating from the
girl's body, like the heat from a light bulb. The smell of fresh

paint has been replaced by a perfumed scent, like freshly cut flowers.

"Hi again," I finally say.

"Hi, Aubrey," she says. Or maybe she doesn't say it, but I hear it all the same. Where her face should be is only a cloud of opaque darkness, so I don't know where the words come from, really.

"You're not … going to hurt me, are you?"

"No."

"OK. That's good." I hesitate. "You called me Aubrey."

"It's your name, isn't it?"

"Yes," I say. I guess she doesn't really understand. "Um, I go by Rosie these days."

"OK, Rosie. What should we do?"

"What?" I can't think what she could possibly mean.

"Can we be friends?"

I pause. I don't know how to be friends with a shadow girl.

"I guess so."

"OK," she says. "I would like that."

She seems curious, yet afraid of me. I think she's more afraid than I am.

"So … where do you come from?" I say.

She doesn't answer for a few seconds. "I can't remember," she says.

"Oh," I respond. I think for a moment. "Are you … me? Some version of me?"

"You're the only you, Rosie," she says.

"Ha," I say. "I guess that's a good thing."

"I like you. I like that you're you."

A tear rolls down my cheek. It's nice to hear something like that right now. Even from a shadow.

"Thanks," I say. "I … like you, too."

"I'm glad," she says.

I smile at her and then yawn. I'm suddenly overcome with exhaustion. "I'm … kind of tired," I say.

"Rest, then," she says, softly.

I curl up on the floor, as I was before. But before long, I feel myself float upwards. I hear the door open and I move backwards through it, my arms and legs limp in the night air. I see the door to the apartment close as I drift back home. Before long, I'm laying in my own bed. I sleep well for the first time in a while.

CHAPTER 16

Even though I'm still the same ol' no-friends Rosie, it doesn't bother me anymore — at least not for the moment.

I haven't been able to stop thinking about the girl in apartment 301. I keep turning over what's happened so far. Both times I've seen her, it's been in the middle of the night. It could've been a dream. *It had to have just been my subconscious, right?*

But that doesn't ring true. I could feel her presence there physically — the warmth surrounding her, the smell of fresh flowers, the lightness I suddenly feel when she's around. Everything changes when she's there. It's like something overtaking my entire body.

I could just forget about her. She hasn't been back to see me in my room. But I'm too curious to leave it alone. And I haven't learned about the others. The figure standing at the end of my bed. The sounds emanating from underneath Mr. Ennis' apartment. I have to know what's happening. And only she can tell me.

Unfortunately, summoning her isn't easy.

One weekend, I try the door during the day. It's already unlocked, so I go in, but Mr. N is in there.

"What you doing in here, mama?" he asks me. I can't really explain myself, so I just mutter that I'm looking for Jimmy and close the door quickly. He seemed annoyed that I'm snooping around. At least the door was unlocked — he still doesn't know I have the key.

So, I decide I can't go in there during the day. I have the feeling that not much will happen during the day, anyway. She'd be invisible to me. I try again one evening, just after dinner. But Dad's around, so I don't feel comfortable staying for more than a few minutes without some sort of excuse, and I'm a terrible liar. He's been around a lot more lately, just when I don't really want him there. *Maybe his little girlfriend is sick of him or something.*

Before long, someone could move in and ruin my chance to find out what's going on. I have to do something now. So, one Saturday night, I tell Dad I want to hang out in my room all night. To avoid seeming suspicious, I blast my Elastica CD and take out a sketch pad. I'm not really drawing or doing much of anything, though. Once 11 rolls around, Dad finally stops puttering around the apartment and reorganizing his pages and goes to bed. Once I see his lights turn off, I wait until it's exactly 11:47. It's now or never.

I walk softly into the other room, open the front door and walk out without making much of a sound. I congratulate myself on not being a klutz for once. Looking out over the railing, I see only a couple of lights on in the windows, and the blinking lights of someone on the second floor watching The Tonight Show. *Ew, Jay Leno*, I think. I scurry across the hall before anyone notices me till I'm right in front of 301.

I grab the key from my pocket and put it into the keyhole, but it's no use. The door doesn't unlock. I twist with all my might, but I'm afraid I'll break the doorknob, so I give up. Mr. N must have changed the locks already. I sit with my back against the door for a few minutes, unsure what to do next. I look at my Guess watch. 11:58.

"I guess I missed my chance," I say aloud. I rest my head in my hands, wondering if I'll ever see the Shadow Girl again.

Only a few moments pass before I feel warmth on my back, as if a fire's started on the other side of the door. I get up, grasp the handle and twist. This time, the door moves weightlessly, as if opening itself.

Inside, the apartment is the same as before. I take my place on the carpet and sit, awaiting her arrival.

This time, it takes only a few seconds for her to appear. Her light glows faintly down the hall.

"There you are," I say.

She doesn't answer me. I give her a second.

"It's OK," I tell her.

"You came back."

"Yeah. I mean, I had to."

"Thank you, Rosie."

"Um, sure. No problem."

She floats toward me. She seems different, off somehow. Her light and her warmth are weaker than before, and I can barely hear her. It's like listening to the ocean through a windowpane.

"Is it ... hard for you to be here?" I ask.

"It's all right. I want to be here. I want us to be friends."

"Yeah," I say. "Me too."

"I'm so glad."

"I just ... hope you're OK."

"You're a nice person, Rosie."

"Thanks. I — I don't feel that nice sometimes."

"I wish I could do more."

"What do you mean?"

"I can't … be here with you like a real person."

"Why not?"

"I … can only do so much."

"Are you …" I stop. I know what I want to ask, but I don't know how to. She seems so frail. "Are you … not here because … you're … dead?"

She barely moves, hovering near me. She says nothing, lowering her head.

"I guess … it's OK, either way," I say.

"I wish I were alive. So we could play together."

"Yeah," I say, thinking how odd it is that she would want to play, like we were little kids. The thought is comforting, though. I've had about enough of the seventh grade at the moment. "I wish we could play, too."

"We could try."

"OK."

"Lie down," she says.

I do as I'm told. I close my eyes for a bit. Nothing seems to be happening, so I open them and sit up. She's gone. But the door to the bedroom opens slightly. Not knowing what else to do, I get up and walk toward it.

I open the door and step into a brightly lit home. Sun filters through the window and illuminates crisp, black leather couches that sit neatly against bright white walls. A brand-new, large TV sits in the family room. Everything gleams with new-ness, lightness, ease, warmth.

My slippers sink into soft, white carpeting. I walk slowly, taking it all in. *Where the heck am I?*

I feel along the white walls and turn a corner, but then find myself back in the same room with the black couches. Or another room just like it.

A white staircase rises in the middle of the room. I hear a giggle from above.

"Rosie," a voice says. It's the Shadow Girl — only her voice sounds different now. Livelier. More human. Familiar, even.

"Hi!" I call up. My voice echoes through the house, bouncing off the angled ceiling. I stare up. Far above, a skylight allows light and warmth to shine onto my face. It feels wonderful.

"Come up," I hear her say.

I do what I'm told and walk up, holding the railing.

"Let's play hide and go seek," she says. I still can't see her. I hear her footsteps going up another set of stairs.

"You're it!" she says, giggling.

I follow, faster. "I'm not really playing yet," I say, trailing her by a stairwell's length. I keep climbing. And climbing. I go up maybe four sets of stairs before I reach another long, white hallway.

At the end of it, a girl in a bubblegum-pink dress with a satin bow stands in front of a closed door. Her dirty blonde hair is shoulder length. She giggles but looks away from me.

I'm out of breath, but I finally catch up to her.

"Is that … you?" I ask. But she doesn't turn to face me. I reach out and touch her back.

"You got me!" she says.

She turns around to reveal a blank, porcelain white face. No eyes, no mouth, but piercing laughter comes from God knows where. I gasp and fall backward. With slow, jerking movements, she moves with insect-like precision toward me.

"What … are you? What's happening?" I say. My voice comes out as a hoarse whisper, as if I have the flu.

She giggles and reaches out to touch me. I get up, and a paw, hard like plastic, reaches forward and lands on my collar bone.

"Ow!" I cry out, swatting away her heavy hand.

"You got me again!" I hear her call out. "I'll get you back!"

I turn and run down the hallway, down the stairs as quickly as I can, with her trailing not far behind. And then another set of stairs. And another. I'm sweating and dizzy from running downward in circles. I leap down the last set of stairs and land back in the room with the black couches. My ankle shoots pain through me, but I ignore it and press on.

The TV is on, and "Andy Griffith" is playing. I turn the corner and climb down another set of stairs, and another, and another. My legs feel like they'll fail me at any second, but when I turn around, I only see the girl's blank, eyeless face coming toward me, a small indentation where a mouth should be, laughing mindlessly as she continues her chase. I turn and continue running down the stairs.

"Stop!" I cry.

She laughs harder and more shrilly as she continues down the stairs.

"I don't want to play anymore!" I call over my shoulder. I finally land back in the same family room. "Mr. Ed" is playing on the TV set. I don't know why, but I rush to the TV and find a remote sitting on the couch. I try to change the channel. *What else can I do?*

The channel changes and it's "The Real World." Puck is picking his nose.

Again, and it's "Mary Tyler Moore."

Again, to "Rugrats."

One more time. The TV changes to the view of a girl, sitting with her back against a door. Her head is down, and she looks injured. She's moaning, and her head bounces up and down with little, spastic motions. Drool froths at her mouth.

I look to my right, where a mirror hangs on the wall.

I don't even recognize myself.

The girl appears behind me in the reflection, descending the last few steps, slowly. Her feet thump down hard.

I look back to the TV set. I see the Shadow Girl, looking as she did before and staring straight at me. A faint sound comes from the TV.

"The front door."

I look to my left to see a white door hidden in the wall, with the faintest outline of light at its edges. I rush toward it, push it open, and run outside. My back arches away from the front door of the apartment. I jump to my feet and stand breathing heavily, sweat dripping down my face and dampening my oversized Indiana University T-shirt.

I lean against the railing, catching my breath. I can still feel pulsing from running down those stairs. I turn around, but there's only the closed door of apartment 301 behind me. I try the handle, and it's cold, locked. *I must have just fallen asleep against the door.*

Over my shoulder, I hear soft crying. I turn around, half expecting to see *her* right behind me. But the sound is coming from one floor down. I go to the railing and look down.

It's Mr. Ennis. It's dark out, but I know it's him. He's standing outside his apartment in his robe and slippers, crying softly to himself. I see the shadows of wisps of hair rising and falling. He leans on the railing as if it's supporting his weight.

I stand watching him. He's so completely consumed by his sadness that he doesn't notice me there, breathing heavily and staring at him from the stairway above. *It's only a matter of time before he does.*

I quietly walk back to my apartment before he has a chance to notice me. Before I know it, I'm back in my bed, tossing and turning in the middle of the night. *I can't even remember going to bed. Was all of it a dream?*

I touch my collar bone, where she touched me. I stiffen as dull pain shoots through my upper body. My ankle throbs from jumping down those endless stairs. I close my eyes and try to put the image of the white doll girl and Mr. Ennis out of my mind. When I shut my eyes, I can still hear the echoes of Mr. Ennis' soft whimper and the girl's laughter. I vow to myself not to ever go back into apartment 301.

CHAPTER 17

Back at school, I try to put my thoughts of the Shadow Girl out of my mind. The few times I've seen her, she's asked me how I was doing, how my day was, making me feel better about myself. But that last time …

I decide that whatever it is, it's not worth it. *It's not real, anyway. You need real people, Rosie. I have to try to change my situation.*

I start striking up more random conversations at school. Even if I seem awkward, I don't care anymore. One day, putting myself out there more finally gets me somewhere.

Señora Chang has us each do a three-minute presentation in Spanish on our interests — what makes us unique, that kind of stuff. We're treated to presentations about riding horses, aspiring actresses, jocks, dancers, video games. When it's my turn, I don't dare talk about any of the things that *really* make me unique — my dead mother, being from a deeply uncool Midwestern town or seeing weird crap in the middle of the night. Instead, I talk about my tape collection.

"I spend all my money on tapes. I'm not that into clothes or anything, obviously," I say in Spanish, pointing to my mom's old jeans that I tore at the knees, my faded Hole *Live Through This* T-shirt and my imitation Docs from Target. That gets a laugh. I show my favorites — Stone Temple Pilots, Smashing Pumpkins and Nirvana, plus some new ones like The Offspring and 10,000 Maniacs that Dad let me buy recently. One kid asks what my favorite song is. I've moved on from "Plush" by Stone Temple Pilots, but I haven't decided on a new one, so I just list a few other favorites — "Zombie" by the Cranberries, "In Bloom" by Nirvana and one of the songs Vera showed me, "When the Levee Breaks" by Led Zeppelin. I play bits of songs on Señora Chang's tape player. When I'm done, I no longer feel like the unpopular loser of the past three months, but the slightly mysterious (if not exactly popular) girl with good taste in music. I can live with that.

"Have you thought about learning to play an instrument?" Señora Chang asks.

I think about her earlier suggestion, about joining band. "Yeah. I wanna learn guitar and start a band one day."

"Yeah, right," Emily says.

"Emilia, I'm docking you for that comment," Señora Chang retorts. Emily crosses her arms.

Suddenly I feel something happen inside me, like a switch going off. I change back to English. "Maybe you could teach me how to play something, Emily," I say. "Do you play guitar or anything? No? You just cheerlead?"

A few of the boys go "Oooh." Señora Chang gives me a sideways glance, and I sit down.

After I'm done, Alex Riojas turns around and says, "Hey, that was pretty cool how you got Emily back like that."

I'm dumbfounded. He's sat in front of me for four months, but none of my pen-borrowing has done a thing to capture his attention. He looks at me, his eyes deep, brown pools, his smile warm, his teeth glimmering white under the fluorescent school lights.

I only realize I'm staring at him when he laughs.
"Since you always borrow my pens, can I borrow one of your tapes sometime? My mom is super Christian and doesn't let me get any good music."

"Sure, you can take one right now," I say, a little too eagerly.

"Thanks. Which one can I borrow?"

"Uh, actually take this mix I made. It has a lot of the bands I like, and you can decide from there."

"Thanks, that's really cool of you. "

"Yeah, well, I'm pretty cool," I say. *Oh God, Rosie, shut up.*

He starts laughing. "Hey, what are you doing after school?"

I'm in shock. I thought at best I'd have a new class friend, not be asked out. "Nothing. I'm not doing anything."

"Cool, have you heard of yearbook?"

Oh. He's not asking you out, dummy. My heart sinks a bit, but I act interested. "Yeah, I mean, I know what it is. Señora Chang told me about it."

"Yeah, she's the teacher. It's kind of lame. I wanted to work on the school newspaper, but they don't have it anymore. This is like the next best thing. Anyway, we're looking for more people to join. If you feel like coming to a meeting, show up in Room 301 at 2:30."

I flinch for a second. "301?"

"Sorry, 321. Ha, sorry, I almost sent you to the wrong room!"

"Yeah! Gosh, that woulda sucked. Well, cool, I guess, I'll check it out, maybe."

"Rosita! Rubio!" Señora Chang says.

"Lo siento!" I say. Alex giggles, and I melt a little bit. We turn back to the front where Nora Nagy, the only girl in the seventh grade more disliked than me, is wearing full Hungarian dress and is doing a traditional dance with a lot of spins. I guess her family is from Hungary. But she's not so good at the dance. Her hand accidentally knocks over the tape player. Twice. The first time, a few people giggle. The second time, everyone erupts in laughter, including Alex. I laugh too, although I feel bad for her.

Leaving class, Alex says, "See you later, Rosie!" and waves.

"Yeah, cool! Catch you," I say. *What?*

I can barely process what happened. *A cute boy almost kinda sorta asked me out. Why did it take me so long to try?*

I look toward the corner of the room where Nora Nagy is stuffing her dress into a bag, tears in her eyes. I had thought about trying to become friends with her before, since neither of us seemed to have any, but she always looked so … angry. But after the attention from Alex, I feel newly confident. I walk over to her.

"Hey, do you need some help?" I ask her.

"Leave me alone!" she cries, storming off in her jeans and Hungarian folk shoes.

"Jeez," I say. But I don't really blame her after how everyone laughed at her, including me. I put Nora out of my mind and start thinking about Alex again as I walk toward the locker hall. I'm daydreaming about bleached-blonde spikes when I hear a voice behind me say, "So do you think you're like rocker girl now or something?"

It's Emily. I turn around. She's barely looking at me as she stands with her hips at a tilt and her hands twirling the pom pom she brought for her dumb cheerleading presentation, as if she can hardly be bothered to annoy me.

"No. I dunno. I just like music."

Emily snorts and walks past me toward the locker hall, her stupid pigtails bouncing on her backpack. *What's her problem, anyway? Maybe she's just jealous because she's so boring,* I think. But even she can't get to me right now. I'm riding high again.

CHAPTER 18

Yearbook turns out to be pretty great. I'm early, so Alex introduces me to a few people and shows me around. He seems to be friendly with a few other girls, but I don't think he likes any of them in that way.

I know the room it's in pretty well — Room 321 is the all-purpose art room. I was too embarrassed to take art because I didn't want to show anyone my drawings, but sometimes I just look into the room like a weirdo and run away the second anyone notices me, so this is a change in three ways: cute guy, cool teacher and getting to be in the art room. It can't get any better.

We're both early. Alex asks Señora Chang something, and then he leads me through a door at the back of the room. He flips on the lights, and everything glows red. Pictures of the campus and students are strung up on wires around the room, and it feels tight and menacing.

"This is the darkroom," he says. "Do you like photography?"

"Yeah, I love it," I say without really thinking about it.

"Cool. Some kids just use this place to hang out or make out when no one's around, but we could use more people who are into taking pictures."

"That's funny," I say, awkwardly laughing. "I mean, hanging out and making out is cool and all, but I think I could take some cool pictures."

He shuts off the light before we leave, and I nervously inch out the doorway. *Calm down, Rosie. Just be cool.*

Once yearbook starts, I'm a little horrified by my first assignment. I'm supposed to interview the other students and ask questions like (seriously) "What do you want to be when you grow up?" I suggest changing the last half of the question to "when you get older." I'm nervous about the assignment, but Señora Chang says that since I'm new, it would be a great way to get to know more people. It occurs to me later that this was also probably the last assignment left that no one else wanted to do.

When we walk out of yearbook, Alex beams his toothy smile at me. His hair is extra spikey today. He looks like an adorable blonde porcupine.

"You did great, Rosie. You'll be a good fit with this crew."

"Thanks. I don't know how I'm gonna do at being the next Connie Chung, though."

"I think you'll be fine. Just be confident. Say it's for a project."

Alex makes everything sound so easy. Of course, it would be for him. He's about the only kid I know who could survive being harassed by some of the popular boys about his hair and still seem cooler than everyone else.

I decide to go out on a limb. "Where do you eat lunch?"

"Usually by the vending machines in the back corner of the quad. You should come by tomorrow."

Yes!

I'm practically skipping when I walk to the bus. I can hardly believe my luck, as if all the bad things that have happened to me were just a trial or something. I feel like I earned this moment.

On the bus, I watch two kids holding hands a couple of seats in front of me. They're eighth graders. The girl is pretty; the guy, not so much. I can't tell if they're popular or what. The eighth grade is so foreign to me, and to all of us in seventh. I feel like they can sense me watching them. The girl sweeps the boy's blond locks from his face to reveal a brace-filled smile. I stare out the window at the passing houses to give them some privacy.

Watching them, I realize I can't tell what Alex wants from me. I'm hardly cool, but Alex isn't your typical guy. *Maybe he does like me.*

I start drawing a heart on the bus window with my finger. I think about writing our initials together, but I change my mind and quickly when I see one of the snot-nosed six graders staring at me. I make it into a Smashing Pumpkins "SP" heart before he says anything, adding a NIN logo for good measure. The truth is, I'm not sure what I'm feeling other than excitement. I'm not sure that I like him like that yet. I think I just really need a friend, and he's the first person who's made an effort.

Back at home, Dad's actually there, for once. He notices me humming the melody to "Today."

"Hey honey, you seem chipper today," he says.

"Thanks," I try to say sarcastically, but I can't hide my smile.

"Making new friends?"

"Maybe a couple. I think I'm gonna join yearbook."

"Atta girl. I knew you'd start to fit in."

Start to fit in. I repeat the phrase in my head. "Yeah, well there are some nice people among all the a-holes."

"Hey, watch the language," Dad says awkwardly.

"Sorry?" I say. He's never really cared about that sort of thing until now, all of a sudden. *I wonder what he's up to …*

"Well, I'm glad for you. Your dad will worry less about you if he knows you're happy at school."

"I didn't think you worried," I say.

"Honey, of course I worry. All dads worry," he says.

"OK."

"And since you're making your own friends now, I think it might be a great time for you to meet some of Daddy's."

Gross. What is he talking about? "Um, OK," I say.

"Your dad has a special new friend in particular, Alison, that he'd love you to meet."

"Dad, why do you keep talking about yourself in the third person?"

"I just think you guys would get along great!"

"Yeah, I'm sure, I didn't say that we wouldn't, I was just asking ..."

"Rosie, just give it a chance, will you?"

There he goes again. Just when things seem like they're looking up, he has to ruin everything. Great, so he has a girlfriend, and I immediately have to meet her.

"Fine. Whatever," I say softly.

I go to my room and barely come out the rest of the night. Dad asks if I'm hungry, and I say no, even though I am. I'm not really even doing anything except pretending to read *The Giver* and sketching little tendrils in the spine of the book. Really, I'm thinking about Alex. *I wonder what he'll think about my mixtape? Which song will be his favorite? He probably won't even listen to it. Alison's a dumb name.*

Even though my mind is restless, I start to get tired, so I change quickly and get into bed. Before long, I'm asleep, but it's one of those light sleeps again. When my eyes blink open a little, I have no idea what time it is, and it seems weirdly light out for the middle of the night. The shadows of sycamore move gently across the closet door, but then start to shudder quickly. *Not now,* I think. I shut my eyes again, but I hear a light shuffling from somewhere inside my room. My eyes open fully. I don't see anything. *Maybe it was nothing this time.*

I roll over and stare out the window. The tree isn't moving. I sit up and see the same thing as before: shadows fluttering across the closet door. "No," I whisper. But it's too late. The shadows converge into a single, writhing mass.

I had almost put her out of my mind. I'd told myself it could've been my imagination, or a dream. The past couple of weeks have been so different, so much better, that I thought I was over whatever it was that was happening to me. But it isn't over. I know that now.

"Rosie," the girl whispers as her undulating, elongated shape comes into view.

"Why are you here?" I ask.

"I didn't see you again. I missed you."

My mind scans back to the last time I saw her. The insane laughter of the faceless girl chasing me down an endless set of stairs.

"Yeah, well, you really scared me the last time," I say with a shudder.

"I'm sorry."

"What are you even doing here?" I ask. "Why do you keep appearing?"

She hesitates, then says, "To warn you."

"Warn me? Of what? After what you did to me ..."

"It wasn't me."

I sit staring at her for a moment longer. "It was … another one?"

"Yes. Another one … intercepted. It's my fault. I just … wanted to be close to you. To protect … my friend."

The Shadow Girl's long, spindly arms and tendrils of hair stop moving. For a moment, she looks like any old shadow cast on the wall.

"Who was it, then?"

"The evil one."

Her voice comes out shrill, her frightened voice echoing through my skull. The room loses its customary warmth and becomes icy. I gather the comforter around me, but the cold cuts through, as if it's coming from within me.

Tears well in my eyes. "Evil one?"

"He is here, too." She begins moving toward me. Her long fingers reach toward me, the shadows growing longer until they're practically caressing my face. "I want to help you. But I can't unless you …"

I scream and try to smack her hand away. My hand moves through hers, and pain lashes at my palm, like touching ice so cold it burns.

"Can't you just leave me alone?" I cry as I leap out of bed. "I have friends now. I don't need you to warn me. I don't need you!" I jump out of bed and turn on the light. I look toward my bed, toward the closet door, toward the window. Of course, there's nothing there now.

I look down at my hand and see a stain that looks like ash across my hand. Slowly, the marks vanish right. I leap back into bed with the lights on, and cover my face with the pillow, sobbing into it freely. *I don't care if Dad can hear me. I hope he does.*

CHAPTER 19

I wake up exhausted, feeling like something is deeply wrong. But I convince myself for the time being that this is normal. I think back to the two times Aunt Rita took me to see a psychologist after Mom died. I remember seeing another girl around my age, maybe a year older, in the waiting room. I wondered why she was there, if she also had a parent who died. *Maybe this is normal,* I think. *Maybe lots of people see things like this, but no one talks about it.*

To his credit, Dad notices something is off about me on the way to school. I tell him I've been having strange dreams lately.

"What kind of dreams? Something about home?"

"No, it's not really like that. I don't even know if they're dreams."

"Of course they are, honey. You've been through a lot this year, and that's OK. Everything is OK."

If you're so concerned, then why are you already dating someone less than a year after Mom died? "If you say so, Dad."

We ride the rest of the way in relative silence. When we arrive, I get out and Dad rolls down the window and calls out over the Chevy's hum, "I'm sorry, Rosie. We can have you meet Alison another time. I'm sorry I brought it up."

He drives off before I have a chance to respond. *Cool way to leave, Dad. At least I have seeing Alex to look forward to.*

*

I do this trick when I'm eagerly waiting for something. I close my eyes tightly for a few seconds and hope that when I open them, time will have somehow passed more quickly. I'm doing this in Science second period, waiting for lunch to come.

"Didn't get enough sleep last night, Rose?" Mr. Minogle asks me as he passes out worksheets. Mr. Minogle looks like a meeker, nerdy version of my dad. He always says Rose, instead of Rosie, which I guess is fine because of my stupid nickname.

Before I know it, it's lunch time, so I guess my trick worked.

"Hey, what's up?" I offer, trying to sound casual as I walk up to Alex, who's sitting near the vending machines. I haven't brought a lunch, but the line looked long, and I didn't want to miss this chance. I expect to see a group of guys that look like Alex and some cool girls. Instead, it's just him and one other person, Jane Kim, a girl from my Algebra class.

"Hey," she says a little coldly.

"Oh hey, Rosie! How's it hangin'?" Alex says cheerily.

"Not much. I mean, it's OK."

"Do you wanna sit?"

"Yeah."

I'm still feeling shaky from the night before, but I make myself socialize and learn a little bit about each of them. Alex is from some place called Van Nuys and lives with his mom. His parents are divorced. He's already listened to my mixtape, which could not be more exciting to me.

"So, you made Alex a mixtape?" Jane says.

"Oh, yeah," I reply. "I made one, not *for* him, but I let him borrow it."

"Oh, do you want it back?" Alex asks.

"No, keep it," I say. "It's for you. I mean, you can keep it."

"I'm glad," Jane says. "The last album Alex bought was Green Day like a year ago."

"Really?" I say. "I just figured you knew a lot of music because, well, your hair."

"Nah, I just wanted to piss off my dad," he says. *So cool.*

"Did you just 'so cool'?" Jane asks.

"What?" I say. *Oh crap, did I move my lips when I thought that?*

"Well, anyway, it's good that you did. Someone has to keep him up to date."

"Whatever. You don't listen to that much music," he says.

"You didn't even know who Mariah Carey was," she says.

Jane isn't especially friendly to me. She makes little jokes at Alex's expense, which I think is odd at first but learn is part of their whole "thing." Jane is quiet in class like me. She has short black hair and glasses, and she wears the same Gap sweatshirt almost every day. I hate to say it, but I kind of thought she was just a boring, nerdy girl before.

I try my best to get in with their little clique, which is really just the two of them. Alex seems all too eager to allow this to happen, but Jane is tougher to crack. She talks to me, but she's never really looking at me when she talks, and all her comments seem to tie back to Alex. I realize pretty quickly that she must be in love with him and nervous about me being around. I try to act like just another friend and not flirt with Alex at all.

"Thanks for letting me hang with you guys," I can't help but say at one point. Alex beams at me, and Jane smiles weakly.

CHAPTER 20

That night I'm really excited about how well things are going. Dad lets us order pizza and a liter of Coke, and I can't stop talking about everything that's going on at school. I can see that he's not really paying attention, but I don't care. This is what he wanted, after all.

Unfortunately, all the caffeine keeps me awake half the night. It's Friday, but still. I haven't been sleeping much in general.

I toss and turn a while before finally forcing myself to get up and pee. I look over at my alarm clock — it reads 11:59 p.m. "Ugh," I mutter. "Whatever. I'm not doing anything but watching the 'Road Rules' marathon this weekend."

I don't bother closing the bathroom door since Dad sleeps like a rock. I'm hanging my head down and trying not to become too awake, when I sense movement. I look up but don't see anything.

"Dad?" I whisper. "Don't come over here, I'm peeing."

I don't hear anything. I pull up my pajama pants and take a couple of steps. I hear a *THUMP*, like someone dropping a pile of wet laundry. I stop in my tracks, standing on tiptoe on the cold tile. For several seconds I don't move, then I see a dark figure like a big cat hustle past the open bathroom door and into the main room without making a sound.

I gasp. *Is it her? It couldn't be. What if it's … him? The 'evil one'? I have to know.*

I walk out and into the main room. The carpet feels hot where feet have left impressions in the carpet. They look like two-toed hoof prints left by a large animal. I keep walking into the other room. It's dark, and fluorescent orange light pours through the blinds into a square on the floor. I stop in my tracks. There, in that spot of light sits a boy, crouching in a ball. Only he looks different. His legs bend back like a dog's legs. It's the shadow of a boy, or an animal, or both. The one who was sitting at the end of my bed.

I stare down at him, frozen. He opens two bright blue eyes with no pupils and looks up at me. His eyes glimmer with curiosity.

He can't be evil, I think. *Can he?*

"Who are you?" I ask.

He giggles. "You finally saw me."

I wrinkle my brow. "Have you been ... poking around here lately?"

Laughter again. "You really are a bit slow, Rosie."

"Hey!"

"... so slow that I bet you can't catch me!"

He bolts out the front door, which I notice is wide open. I chase after him as he bounds down across the floor and down the stairs. I haven't thought about what I'm doing or why, and haven't even put on slippers or shoes. At the bottom of the stairs, I see him crouching in the shadow of the back door to the apartment complex, which is open.

"You're good at this game," he says before bolting out the back.

I chase after him. The streetlights cast orange squares onto the sidewalk. No cars drive by as I run beneath the sycamore and into the construction site. Everything is so still that it all feels frozen in time.

I see the boy's dark, gangly body bound through the grass, and he disappears into the pit of mud.

"Be careful," I call out as I follow. I reach down and try to steady myself, but I stumble and roll down the hill into the pit. My head hits the ground, which feels wet before I even notice it's started to drizzle.

He's sitting in the middle of the pit, looking at me with those piercing blue eyes. He starts to sink slowly. *I have to help him.* I try to run but my feet sink deep into the mud with each step, pulling back out slowly. I can't reach him in time. I get close, my fingers reaching toward him before I see his head sink beneath the mud. *There's nothing I can do for him now.*

I turn around and pull my feet out of the mud. The drizzle has turned to a downpour. The rain turns the dirt into thick mud that sticks like molasses to my feet. I sink my hands into the sides of the pit to pull myself up, but every handful and kick sinks me farther into the slop, and I can't make it up past a few inches. I kick my feet even faster, trying to swim upwards, digging my nails into the mud, but the bank gets steeper and steeper until it's a sheer wall. I can't keep up my momentum. I'm sliding downward, then falling, far, down, down … I take a huge breath just before I hit the mud so that I don't drown instantly. I'm sinking farther and farther down, holding my breath and trying to swim through the mud with all of my might … until I suddenly lurch forward in bed, breathing heavily, my back sopping wet with sweat.

I shake my head in my hands and try to make sense of things. *Did I fall asleep in the bathroom and come back to bed?* My hands grip the side of the bed and I look at my alarm clock. It's flashing 12:19 a.m. *Did the power go out?* I look outside and the sycamore branches brush against the window. Light rain pings against the frame.

"Another dream," I say, lying back down. I loosen my grip on the bed and run my thumbs against my fingertips. There's something caked on them.

I look at my right hand to see that my nails are blackened and long. "Gross," I say to myself. "I really need to trim my nails." I notice that it isn't just my nails; my hands are covered in dry mud.

I leap out of bed and run to the restroom. The faucet pours warm water over my hands, rinsing the mud off of them until there's nothing left. I raise my shaking hands in front of my face. I can feel walls within my mind that have been shielding me from the impossibility of all of this now tumbling down.

"It's real," I say.

CHAPTER 21

I'm getting ready in a hurry because I slept in after that last dream — or whatever it was — kept me awake. Dad's been getting back in late from his little dates, too, so we're both running behind. I'm pulling on my favorite pair of Levi's, which keep getting stuck at my thighs lately, but I don't want to get rid of them because they've got the perfect amount of wear at the knees now. I feel completely disheveled. I look over at the shelf at Karen. I need her wisdom now. "Karen, what's wrong with me?" I cry out, trying to make myself feel less crazy. *Nothing like talking to your doll/imaginary friend to take care of that!* I grab her and stuff her in my backpack anyway.

School is beyond a drag. Alex is out sick with the flu, meaning that the one thing I usually look forward to all day can't even get me through. I'm so tired that I actually forget where first period is. When I stumble into Ms. Torres' English class, I can't even muster an excuse. Later, in Science, Mr. Minogle calls me out for trying to be sneaky and listening to my Cranberries tape on headphones through my jacket and under my hair. He usually would have taken it away, but I don't usually do that sort of thing, and I must look pitiful because he takes another look at me and moves on.

But that's not the worst of it. Without Alex there, I feel weird having lunch with just Jane, so I ask Señora Chang if she doesn't mind if I stay and work on some of my Spanish homework again. She lets me, and I get through about three conjunctive phrases in 20 minutes. It's no use; I can't focus. I leave to put my stuff in my locker. Just my luck: there's Lauren, Emily and Mia hanging out in the locker hall — "the treacherous trio," as Alex calls them.

Anyway, I'm preoccupied. I open my backpack and stuff my Spanish book in my locker quickly.

"Hey," Mia calls to me. I look over. "I like your backpack," she says. I look down at my vomit-green Walmart backpack with a giant hole in it that I've had for two years. It doesn't stack up too well with the other girls' brand new JanSports, even with all the band names I've scrawled across it in white-out pen. I realize she's making fun of me.

"Whatever," I say flatly, and start to walk off.

"Hey, where are you going?" Mia asks, walking behind me, flanked by a smirking Emily and Lauren. "I was talking to you."

"Just to class," I say, flipping my head around and then back again to keep walking.

"I said I like your backpack." Mia kicks it, and I tumble forward a bit.

"Stop it," I say, turning my head but still walking.

They keep trailing behind me, and there's no one else in the hall. Mia kicks my backpack again.

"Stop!" I say, my voice cracking.

Emily and Lauren giggle. I start to walk faster but get jerked back as Mia grabs my backpack, which tears as it comes off of me.

I'm forced to turn around. "Give it back!" I say, barely fighting back tears. Mia laughs and throws it to Emily.

"Ew, I don't want this thing!" she says, throwing it to Lauren.

"I don't want it!" Lauren says, dropping my torn backpack on the floor. The rest of my belongings come tumbling out, including Karen.

"Oh my god. Is that a troll doll?" Emily says.

"Let me see," Mia says, picking her up.

"Give it back!" I scream, snatching it out of Mia's hand.

"Hey!" she says angrily, her advantage upset by my fighting back a little. Emily, Lauren and Mia let go of my stuff and erupt in laughter as I try to put everything back into my backpack.

"Rosie O'Donnell still plays with dolls!" Lauren says, as though she can hardly believe her luck at having discovered this about me. They all start walking away down the hall, while I walk the other way, clutching my bag, in tears. Emily catches up to me and places her hands around my shoulders.

"Hey, we're just messing around, right?" she says, as if I'm supposed to have some sort of answer. "Don't go telling Mrs. Sailor."

"Leave her alone, Emily" Jane says, suddenly appearing out of nowhere and pushing her hand against Emily's chest.

"Jeez, I don't know why she's making such a big deal out of it."

"What the hell's the matter with you?" Jane says. Emily shrugs and walks away.

Afterward, Jane takes me into the girls' bathroom and lets me cry a bit. "Are you OK?" she asks after a few minutes.

"Yeah," I mutter. I look up. "The bell rang."

"It's OK, I just have P.E. next. I was looking for you earlier."

"You were?"

"Yeah, duh," she says. "Sorry about those girls. They're the worst."

"I ... hate them," I say.

After a moment's thought, Jane offers, "Did you know Emily

stuffs her bra?"

"What?"

"Yeah. She's in my P.E. class. She totally stuffs."

I start laughing and sniffling at the same time. "Really?"

"Yup. It's so obvious. Ms. Perfect Straight-A's has no boobs. I mean, neither do I, but at least I don't stuff. Every time she changes, she fusses and hides behind the locker door. One time I saw tissue sticking out of her bra. She looked like she was gonna murder me."

I laugh and wipe snot and tears from my face. "Oh no! You have P.E. with her next. Is she gonna sic her friends on you?"

"So what? I'm not afraid of them. Plus, I know who Mia cheats off of in math. She'll never go after me."

After a few moments of silence, Jane really surprises me. "Fuck those girls," she says.

We're best friends from that moment on.

CHAPTER 22

I drag my broken backpack around for the rest of the day. The bus drops me off early, because of construction work, in front of a Wendy's where homeless guys hang out. I clutch my backpack, dropping things along the way as I walk the two blocks to our apartment building.

Mr. N is watering the solitary bird of paradise plant that stands in the middle of our empty courtyard. As soon as I walk in, sweating, I spill my books all over the place. I almost start crying.

"Ah, mama, don't worry. You'll soon grow out of that phase," he says. I guess he means my clumsiness.

"It's fine," I say, trying to shake it off as I gather my stuff.

"Hold on. Hold on," he says. He turns off the hose and scuttles to his apartment. I sit on the floor for a couple of minutes before he comes back out touting a militaristic-looking backpack with hoops and buckles for ... I don't know what they're for.

"Oh, it's OK, Mr. N," I say.

"Nonsense, mama," he says. "I bought this for my son before he went back to the army, but he couldn't take it, so he left it here. I have no use for it — you take it. My gift to you."

When he puts it that way, I can't refuse, so I thank him, transfer my stuff to my new SWAT team backpack and lug it upstairs. It's huge and can fit all my stuff and probably a small dog, too. It's about half my size and practically swallows me, but I don't have a lot of options.

I unlock the door and drop my bomb-squad pack on the floor when I see Dad standing in the kitchen with a perky blonde woman. She has what looks like the Supercuts version of the "Rachel" haircut, which makes her look at lot older than … *God, is she in her twenties?*

"Honey, this is Alison. Remember I was telling you about her?" Dad says.

"Hi," Alison says, beaming and outstretching her cardiganed arm. "It's so nice to meet you. Your dad has told me so much about you."

I pause. "Oh yeah?" I ask. "What has he told you?"

"Oh, just that you're doing well in school, loving it here in L.A.," she says, shrugging her shoulders for emphasis.

"That's right," I say, deadpan. "I'm doing well in school, and I'm loving it here in L.A."

"That's great to hear," she says nervously.

"Honey, where'd you get that backpack?" Dad says.

"Oh, this? Well …" I consider telling him the entire truth, that some mean girls tore apart my crappy backpack, but I decide to save us all the additional awkwardness. "Uh, my backpack broke. Mr. N gave me this thing so I could get my stuff upstairs."

"That was so nice of him," Dad says. "We'll have to thank him for your new backpack."

"It's not my new backpack," I say.

"What's wrong with it?"

"Dad, I can't go to school with this thing! Look at it!"

"Danny, I think a girl like her would want something a little more feminine," Alison offers.

"A girl like me?" I say, defensively. "You don't even know me."

"Rosie!" Dad snaps. "Don't be rude."

"It's OK," Alison says. "Really, it's OK."

I throw the backpack down on the floor and stomp to my room, flopping down on my bed "A girl like her," I repeat. *What the heck does Fake Rachel know?*

Just then, I notice Karen sticking out of my backpack. *What are you doing, Rosie? You bring your doll around with you everywhere you go, and you're surprised when the other girls make fun of you.* I pick the doll up and throw it across the room. It lands with a thud against the closet.

Staring at Karen lying on the floor, I think about Mom. How she always worried about me, how she cared about every little thing. And I just threw one of the only things I have left of her across the room like trash. I start crying and cover my face with a pillow.

I must fall asleep like that, because the next thing I hear is a female voice. "Hello," she says, waking me up.

"Huh? Ugh. Sorry Alison, I had sort of a bad day. Can we talk another time?" I say from under the pillow.

"I'm not Alison," she says.

I pull the pillow off my face and find that everything has changed. It's nighttime, and the room has a faint glow like it's being lit from high above. It smells musty, as if it's been raining. *How long have I been asleep?*

This all registers before I notice the Shadow Girl standing in front of me. Her presence is stronger this time, and her arms and legs are spread out in front of my closet door. My legs instinctively kick until I'm sitting up in bed.

"Sorry," she says. Her voice sounds more human this time. Older. "I know you told me to leave you alone ..."

"Oh," I say, remembering the last time. "I'm sorry. It's just ... I was scared."

"I don't want to scare you."

"What ... happened? The time before?" I ask. I think about the pristine white house. The staircases stretching up endlessly, the rooms that turned into one another.

"I wanted us ... to be able to play together. So you could trust me. But ... he took over."

"That was scary," was all I could think to say.

Her head lowers. "I don't know how ... to be a person anymore."

I stay quiet for a minute, thinking about this. "Well," I say, "I don't really know how to do that, either."

"You have friends now. That's good."

"But ... I ... still want to know you, too."

Her glow brightens at this remark. "OK," she says.

"Last time, you said I was in danger."

She hesitates. "Yes."

"Why? Why does it ... he ... what does he want?"

She holds a hand up to her face as if to silence me. I stare at her, unsure of what to say or do.

"You're not safe anymore. I'm losing myself," she says, raising her long fingers. They trail into the air to disappear like smoke.

"Maybe ... I could just go with you," I say.

"Come with me? To the other place?"

"Yes," I say. "I don't like it here anymore. No one understands me here."

"If you come with me … I could keep you safe."

She floats out of the room, moving along the walls and door. I follow her without thinking. By the time I'm in the living room, she's disappeared. There's nothing there except a couple of opened Cokes on the kitchen counter, the unbearable glow of the fluorescent hall lights pouring in and an open front door that sits still in the dead winter air. I walk outside without closing the door.

I stand staring, stupefied in the corridor. The lights illuminate the metal railing, producing shadows of the bars along the ground. I stare down at them, and the shadows of the bars begin to stretch along the ground, tearing apart from one another and wriggling until they've become something like legs. They move together like tentacles down the corridor and toward the stairway.

I breathe in deeply. The air is so cold and stale that it makes me cough. I follow the wriggling shadows down the stairwell. I can't see much and hold onto the wall as I walk past Mr. Ennis' door and down into the courtyard. When I get to the bottom of the stairs, I take another deep breath and tap my feet three times on the ground. *I'm really here*, I tell myself. "I'm really here," I say aloud.

"This is dumb, Rosie," I say again. *I should just go home.*

I turn to go back upstairs — then I see the Shadow Girl standing in the way. Her long black hair flows straight into her legs and I find it almost unbearable to look at her featureless face.

She turns slowly and flows into the space underneath the stairs. My mind goes blank, but my legs move me to follow, despite my desire to go home. *I know what's at home*, I think. *But I have to know what else there is.*

I'm underneath the stairs, in darkness. When my eyes adjust, I see the Shadow Girl standing in front of the door I saw earlier. Light begins to pour through two slits in the doorway and forms an aura of light around her body. The door opens and she moves inside. I follow.

It's dark inside the room. I stand there, waiting for something to happen. After a few seconds pass, the Shadow Girl's glow grows brighter, exposing the room around us. I expect to see a heater, maybe some cleaning supplies. But the room is empty of objects. Instead I see people.

There is Mrs. N, her golden earrings dangling as she smiles lifelessly at me. Next to her is the Asian mom, holding her two twin boys close to her, still dressed in red rain jackets. Alfonso, the handyman, is standing and blocking the door, stonefaced. My eyes dart around the huddled room. Mrs. Lieberman with a frozen grin, her cats unmoving in her arms. Then Vera, standing with Jimmy, only they don't seem to recognize me. "Hey," I try to call out, but my voice is too weak to be heard.

"What are you all doing here?" I ask. But I don't even hear myself. My voice is empty.

"What is this place?" I try to call to the Shadow Girl. No sound comes out, but she seems to hear me.

"We are in the other place," she says.

Her arms extend like tendrils toward mine. I stare down at my hands, and they're faded, like a half-exposed photograph.

Her hands move closer toward mine.

Soon, they're touching. I can't tell where her hands end and mine begin.

I look around the room again at the people around me, who

129

seems like husks of their real selves. I'm propelled forward by the Shadow Girl, between these people and toward a stairwell. The Shadow Girl is moving upward in front of me. I try to walk, but my legs give way to nothingness. I feel like I no longer exist.

"I don't want this anymore!" I call out silently. I pull back, and slowly, my arm comes back into view. I let go of her.

Now I don't see her at all, up that long stairwell. I feel weak and almost unable to move. My hands fade in and out of existence. I'm crawling upward, one stair at a time, and it's completely pitch black on either side of me. Shadow hands reach through the darkness on both sides and paw at me, almost beckoning me to join them. I crawl up further, the hands continuing to reach out. I can feel them pulling at me, my energy sapping with each touch. *Why can't I move any faster?* I try to breathe, in and out, slowly, moving so slowly …

I finally get to the top and then stand up. I feel exhausted, but I'm able to run down the hallway, away from the stairwell. The white walls around me seem strangely familiar. That stale smell … it's the hallway in our old house. I see the Shadow Girl moving toward a closed door. I can't keep up with her, though, and the hallway seems to stretch for miles. She glides underneath the door like smoke. *I have to reach her.* When I grasp at the door handle it burns my hand.

I fall to the floor and rest my head for a moment, my energy completely drained.

I see something. An open door. Mr. Ennis is inside. My body is light, half shadow, half flesh. I'm floating over him as he's sitting in his recliner, smoking a cigar. He smiles as he bites down on it. What's left of body melds into the smoke and floats upward, out the window and into the night sky. I'm falling upward, faster and faster, disintegrating into nothingness.

The next thing I know, I'm back in my room, wiping sweat and hair from my face. My heart is racing like I just ran a mile at full speed. I lay back down, feeling weak and confused. I reach my arms forward and see dark handprints slowly fading across them. Breathing deeply, I can still smell the cigar smoke lingering in my nostrils.

CHAPTER 23

The next day, I'm utterly wiped. Ms. Torres is going on about the latest chapter of "Huck Finn" that I was supposed to read last night before falling asleep. I can't focus, and I have no idea what she's talking about anyway, so I pull the drawstrings of my hoodie closed over my face and put my head in my hands. I've seen some of the grungy stoner kids do it a million times. Why can't I?

Through my muffled little catacomb, I hear Ms. Torres going on about the significance of the dead body in the frame house Huck and Jim see on the river. I usually love English, but I couldn't care less at this point. I drift off.

Then something strange happens: I see Mom. I've been waiting to dream about her all this time, and I finally get to see her. It's nothing special. We're at the house in Galena. She's sitting on our old couch, knitting. It's this old wicker couch with green cushions with patterns of leaves all over them. She was always complaining that she wanted a new couch, a new house, but I loved falling asleep on that couch, even though it wasn't that comfortable.

I walk into the room from the tiled entryway, stepping onto soft, white carpet. I try to sink my feet in with each step, enjoying how lush it feels. Mom's head is lowered, and she's dressed in a long, red dress, something old-fashioned that she would never wear in real life. Her dirty blonde hair covers her face as she knits. *Mom always hated knitting*, I think. She said her mom always made her do it with her on Sunday nights after supper. I never got the chance to learn.

"Can I sit with you?" I ask her.

"Of course, honey," she says, without lifting her head.

I sit beside her and stare at her. She's completely focused and humming something I've never heard her hum before. Other than that, it's so quiet that I can hear the soft gurgling of a pot boiling on the stove in the kitchen.

"Mom?" I ask with tears in my eyes. "Can … you teach me?"

She doesn't reply. I reach out to touch her hands, but she's suddenly not there. *Of course she's not there*, I think as I open my eyes. I undo my hoodie and sit up. The class is empty. *How long was I asleep?*

I look up at the clock. The numbers are unrecognizable, and the hands have stopped moving. Out of the corner of my eye, I see something moving in the doorway. But there's no one there.

"Ms. Torres?" I ask. Nothing. "Is that you? Sorry … I'm not feeling very well." I rub my eyes and shuffle in my seat.

Then I see it: an elongated splatter of a shadow stretching against the classroom wall. It oozes across the whiteboard and toward the chairs. Then the shadow peels off the wall and starts to form into something.

It's her. She stands in front of me.

"Rosie," she says.

"What are you doing here?" I ask.

"You have to be careful."

"You told me," I say. "But … what were you trying to show me? You … scared me again."

"You have to try to see. You can't resist. You have to—"

The girl's soft voice cuts out. Her back arches, and her long hair shortens. Her body elongates, and her dress splits into two thin legs, bent backwards like an insect's. Her head becomes long and oblong, almost crescent-shaped. Her soft voice becomes gruffer. A low growl … it's something I've heard before. It's inhuman.

I get up and back up against the wall, but there's nowhere to go. I run past the grotesque shape and out the door. I look around; there's no one in sight. The adjoining classrooms are dark and abandoned. I look behind me and see that the shape has fully formed to become a tall man. He turns his head around and stares at me with lifeless sockets for eyes.

I don't wait around to find out what he wants. I start to run away, but my feet pedal in the air. I can barely propel myself. I look back and see that he has begun to move toward me with sharp, rigid movements. He moves slowly but deliberately toward me as I'm flailing helplessly.

My foot finally catches on the ground. I run toward the locker hall. *Don't look back*, I tell myself. But I do. He floats toward me, his dark claws outstretched and his mouth agape. He grows larger and larger, around my entire body, swallowing me whole.

I wake up and gasp. Ms. Torres' hand is on my shoulders. "Rosie, what on earth are you doing?" she says, and the class erupts in laughter. I stare around the room and see Emily staring at me, smiling without so much as a snicker. I rest my head back down on my arms.

Alex pokes me from where he sits, across and one seat back. "Are you feeling OK?" he asks.

"Yeah, I'm fine," I say, a little rudely. "Uh, are you feeling better?"

"Me? I'm fine. I just … needed a day off."

"Tell me about it."

Class moves on pretty quickly, and I try to maintain my composure for the remaining 23 minutes.

Ms. Torres is helping someone with a question when Alex leans in again. "Hey, I heard about Emily and those girls," he whispers. *Mortified.* "Emily's such a bitch."

I'm grateful for the sympathy, especially after my little episode, but I also feel weird about him calling her a bitch, even though he's right. She is a bitch. "Oh, I was fine. Jane told you about that?"

"Yeah, I think she was a little worked up. She tries to act tougher than she is. Those girls have given her a hard time, too. I feel like they like to harass all the new girls and anyone who's smarter than them, which is, like, everyone."

This makes me feel better. "Yeah, well, I don't think she's gonna win any brain contests any soon." *OK, awkward comment.* "And I heard she stuffs her bra."

"Rosie!" I hear from the front of the room. Ms. Torres is glaring daggers at me. "Honestly, what's gotten into you?"

"Sorry, Ms. Torres," I say. *Crap, could she have heard what I said? Did Emily? I can't even look at her. Whatever, at least I made Alex laugh, even if that was pretty mean to spread around.*

After class, Alex runs ahead to get to a Pre-Algebra quiz. Ms. Torres reaches out her hand to stop me, and I almost jump out of my skin.

"Rosie," she starts. "Sorry, I didn't mean to scare you."

"Oh, sorry I fell asleep and all that. It won't happen again."

"I'm concerned," she says. "How are you holding up?"

"Um, I'm fine. I'm liking it here better now. I made a few friends."

"I can see that. That's good," she says. "Alex is a nice kid. But I'm more worried about you in particular. I don't know about other classes, but you're getting an A in this one. You shouldn't be falling asleep in class like that."

"Oh yeah," I say. I really am exhausted and can't think of anything else to say.

"Is everything OK at home?"

"Mmm hmm," I say.

"I don't mean to pry. I just want you to know that I'm here in case you need to talk." She pauses and adjusts her glasses. I stare blankly at her square-shaped hairdo. "Here," she says and begins to write something down on a post-it. "Take this note to the office and see Mrs. Sailor."

"Oh, that's OK. I don't want to bug her."

"I know she seems tough, but she's a smart lady. She's a trained psychologist, you know." She stops, and I can see her considering her words, although I'm too out of it to really be phased by any of this. "She's a great listener. I'd really like for you to go speak with her."

"Thanks, Ms. Torres," I say, trying to appear earnest as I take the post-it. "I'll get right on top of that."

"*I'm right on top of that, Rose,*" I whisper to myself. It's a line from "Don't Tell Mom the Babysitter's Dead," one of my favorites. I laugh a little.

"What was that?" Ms. Torres asks.

"What?" I realize I've been talking to myself out loud.

"You said something. Was that to me or to yourself?"

"Oh." I shake my head. "It was nothing. It was just this thing from a movie that sounded like—"

"Rosie," she says. "I'm telling you to please go speak with Mrs.

Sailor. It's not a question anymore. You can do it on your own time, but I'll let her know, and she'll be expecting you. OK, go to your next class, then."

I walk out feeling horrified. *Could this day get any worse? At least I have something to tell Alex and Jane at lunch: Ms. Torres thinks I'm crazy. She might be right, though.*

When I leave class, I see Emily and Lauren whispering and giggling. Nothing unusual, but to my surprise, Emily breaks away and walks toward me. "Hey, Rosie," she says.

"Yeah?" I ask, annoyed.

"What did Ms. Torres want?"

"What?"

"I saw her talking to you. You weren't tattling on us, were you?"

"No. What? No, she was just mad at me because I fell asleep."

"Oh, OK. Why are you so tired, anyway?"

"Uh, I just didn't sleep good."

"Oh my God, look at her backpack!" Lauren says, pointing at the hooked monstrosity on my back.

"Well, I needed *something*," I say.

Emily ignores this comment, knowing it reflects poorly on her. "Did you know Ms. Torres is a lesbian?"

"What? Really?"

"Yeah. Why, does that excite you?" Emily asks, while Lauren giggles.

"No. I mean, I don't care."

"Sure," Emily says. "It's fine if you're gay. You and Alex could start a club or something."

"I'm not gay and shut up about Alex!" I shout. I can feel the tears welling up again.

"Jeez, I was just kidding," Emily says, playing with her pigtails. "You don't have to go all Courtney Love on me."

I turn and stomp away, wiping away tears. "Bye, Rosie!" Emily calls out to me, and I can hear Lauren's laughter echoing in the halls.

I tell Alex and Jane about the mean girls at lunch.

"She's just jealous because you get better grades than her," Alex offers.

"Girls like that don't care about grades," Jane says.

"Emily does," Alex retorts. "She's really competitive."

"We should get her back," Jane says. "Let's put dog shit in her locker."

"No!" I say, laughing. "I don't want to make her not like me even more."

"Oh, Rosie, why do you care what those girls think?" Jane says. "They're never gonna like you."

This stings. "Why?" I ask.

"That's just how it is."

"Don't be mean," Alex says. "She's still new."

"She's not that new," Jane says. "Some people *just suck*. Those girls *just suck*. I still say dog shit is the answer."

"Maybe," I say, but I'm not really listening. I'm thinking about that horrible dream. That horrible thing I saw chasing me down the hallway. I had almost forgotten about it in the mess with Ms. Torres and Emily.

The rest of the day, I can't stop thinking about it. I try to think about Mom instead. *I saw Mom in a dream, didn't I? I should be happy about that.*

But it feels like something has changed. As if the danger the Shadow Girl was trying to warn me of is moving closer.

CHAPTER 24

The next night, I'm at Jimmy and Vera's for the first time in a while. Although Dad *ever so graciously* invited me to tag along with him and Alison on their date, I told him I'd rather die. OK, not really. I just told him I wanted to spend time with Jimmy and Vera, which is true.

Only now I'm too distracted to be much fun. I'm thinking about what I saw at school and last night in the apartment complex. The Shadow Man, I've dubbed him in my mind. He's not like the others I've seen: the Shadow Girl and the Shadow Boy. They felt strangely childlike. But this one feels … so terrible. Like all the worst things you've ever thought, said out loud at once.

I'm thinking about this tonight as I'm absent-mindedly running Jimmy's racecar on the carpet. I'm surprised he let me play with it at all. It's his favorite thing, and he can be pretty particular about his stuff. To be honest, it's only because he asked to see Karen. He's been teasing her hair and humming to himself for the past five minutes. I don't really know what we're doing, but I know that it feels better being here than being alone with my thoughts.

But that's the funny thing about your thoughts; you can only avoid them for so long.

"Jimmy," I say finally.

He doesn't stop humming or playing with Karen's hair. This is pretty typical for him.

"Jimmy!" I say, a little bit louder than I mean to. He gets startled and looks at me wide-eyed. "Sorry," I say. He goes back to twirling Karen's hair, but the humming has stopped. I take this as a sign that I can continue.

"Do you remember ... when you told me that sometimes you see things that aren't there?"

"Uh huh," he says, without looking up.

"What did you mean by that?"

Jimmy sighs, as if a little bit bothered that he has to explain himself. "Like ... sometimes I think I see someone there, like Aunt Vera. But then I look again and it's no one."

I'm stunned by this. "Me too."

Now Jimmy fixes his attention on me, staring me straight in the eyes. He never does this. "Really?"

"Yeah, really. In the apartment building, mostly."

Jimmy goes back to twirling. For a moment I think he's lost interest, but then he looks me in the eye. "Who do you see?"

"People."

"What people?"

"They're not people. Or they are. I don't know who they are. They all seem to be ... after me somehow."

"I don't understand."

"It's ... shadow people."

After I say that, Jimmy stops fiddling. "Shadow people?"

"Yeah. Shadow people."

"Shadow people ..."

"Yeah. There's a girl, in apartment 301 ..."

"Shadow people!"

"Jimmy, shh!"

"What's going on?" Vera asks, walking in from the kitchen.

"Nothing. We were just playing a game," I lie.

Vera looks at me and then at Jimmy. "Do you guys want to watch a movie?" she asks. I recognize this as a way to avoid one of Jimmy's more difficult moods.

"Nightmare!" he yells.

Visions of my dreams come flooding back. *The faceless girl. The Shadow Man …*

"Jimmy, how many times have we watched 'Nightmare Before Christmas' now?"

"It's OK. I don't mind. I like that movie," I say, eagerly. I'm just happy that Jimmy has moved on from what I've told him, and I instantly regret having said anything.

Vera pops *The Nightmare Before Christmas* into the VCR and is in and out of the room, making Shake 'n Bake for us. Right about the time "Making Christmas" starts in the movie, Vera asks me to help her in the kitchen.

I worry that she's going to scold me for getting Jimmy all worked up earlier. But she doesn't. She's dressed in a yellow button-down blouse and jeans, and her gray-streaked blonde hair is up in a headband. I didn't notice before, but I've never seen her look so … momish. She usually looks a lot closer to how I think an artist or a writer would look — I guess she is a writer, after all.

"Here," she says, handing me a plastic bag full of chicken. "I kind of messed up the first batch. Can you shake this for me?"

"Thanks," I say, taking the bag. "Um … what do I do?"

"You just shake it, lovey. Up and down. Yup, just like that. Did you guys ever eat this back home?"

"No, my mom used to make more, like, stews and pies and stuff. She always had something boiling on the stove."

"Was she a good cook?"

"Yeah. I mean, I never really noticed, but I guess she was. Really good."

"What about your dad? What do you guys usually eat?"

"Uh, just whatever. Spaghetti, mostly. Pizza. TV dinners."

"Ah, and does he cook, or do you help him?"

"I used to help a little, or he'll burn himself and yell a lot. Lately he hasn't, so I just eat a Lean Cuisine or something."

"Huh," she says. "Where's your dad at tonight?"

"He didn't tell you?"

"No, he just said 'thank you' and headed out. I think he was running late. He did look pretty spiffy, though."

"Yeah, he's on a date."

"Oh, is that right?" she says, taking the bag of chicken from me. "How do you feel about that?"

I suddenly realize how much she's been asking me about Dad. *Does she like him? Maybe she's jealous. That's too gross to even think about.*

"Eh," I say. "There's not too much I can do about it. She seems fine. Alison. That's his girlfriend."

"Have you met this girlfriend?"

I think back to the night the Shadow Girl appeared in my room.

"I did. Real quick. She's kind of ..."

"Kind of what?"

"I dunno. She seems dumb," I say. "Sorry, that's not nice, I know."

Vera laughs. "It's OK, doll. I won't say anything."

Doll. The Shadow Girl ... became like a living doll. But it was the Shadow Man. The bruise on my chest ... it's still there.

"Rosie?"

"Huh?" I ask. My hand is touching my chest, and I'm staring blankly.

Vera looks at me intently, but she goes back to shoving the pan of chicken in the oven. "You can always talk to me, love," is all she says.

I go back into the living room and rejoin Jimmy on the couch. We're lying on either side of the brown sectional. Jimmy's hair is splayed out on the pillow next to me. I get the sudden urge to tussle it, but I hold back, knowing that Jimmy doesn't like to be touched.

"Jimmy?" I say.

"Mmm hmm?"

"Why don't you keep Karen?"

"Really?"

"Yeah, really. She's happy here."

Jimmy excitedly clasps her in his hands. Then he does something he's never done before: He reaches over and hugs me. Surprised, I stiffen up, but I relax and hug him back. It only lasts a moment, but I recognize how significant this is for Jimmy.

We go back to lying there together, and I feel the most comfortable I have in a while. I fall asleep before dinner.

*

The next day, I'm feeling well-rested and confident for a change. I decide to extend a fig leaf to Dad.

"How was your date last night?" I ask as genuinely as possible.

Dad's taken aback. "It ... was good, Rosie. It was real good."

"Good," I say.

"You seem ... good, too?"

"Yeah, Dad. I'm good."

"Hey, I haven't seen you carrying around that doll lately. Karen, right? You getting too old for that?"

"I gave her to Jimmy. He was really excited about the doll, and yeah, I am getting too old for it." My thoughts travel back to the real Karen for a moment. "Dad, whatever happened to them? Karen and the neighbors? Why did they move away, anyway?"

Dad's quiet a moment. "Well, your mom and I didn't want to tell you at the time, but ... Karen was very sick. She was dying, sweetie. They moved away because her health was going south."

I'm stunned. "Sick? Like ... Mom sick?"

"It wasn't cancer," he says. "It was ... a thing she was born with. Um, cystic ..."

"Cystic fibrosis," I say, thinking about a made-for-TV movie I loved about a girl with cystic fibrosis that starred the dad from "Coach" and "Poltergeist." I taped it and watched it a few times.

"That's it," he says. "I'm sorry I didn't tell you when you were younger, sweetie. You weren't really old enough to understand."

"Oh," I say. "I can't believe it."

"Sorry, I shouldn't have upset you just before school."

"It's OK," I say. "It was … a long time ago."

CHAPTER 25

At school, I decide to get a jump on my interviews for yearbook — mostly so that I have more to talk about with Alex. I always like to get the worst part of something over with quickly, and I have to talk to everyone in our class. So I walk over to where Emily and her friends are standing on the grass hump between the math and English buildings. I never really go over here, but right now there's Emily and a couple of her friends I don't know. *If I can get them one at a time, maybe it won't be so bad.*

"Hey Emily," I say, flatly.

"Oh hey … Rosie?" she asks. Her friend next to her giggles.

"You know who I am," I say. Emily looks surprised. I pull out a notebook with a cover scrawled with all my favorite bands in whiteout pen. Before she can get her dig in, I continue. "I have to do this dumb thing for yearbook. You want to be in it, right?"

"Uh, yeah," she says, confused.

"OK, so what do you want to do when you grow up? When you get older?"

"Huh?" she asks, still seeming confused.

"You know," I say. "Like, what do you want to do for a job?"

"Oh, well first I want to go to a really good college. Like maybe I can play a sport or something. I dunno, wait, what're you writing? Don't write that down."

"OK," I say.

"Like …"

"Don't you want to be a cheerleader at UCLA?" a girl I don't know asks.

"Shut up, Sarah! You can't be a cheerleader for a job. Um, OK, write this. I always like helping people. Like how you were new, and I always tried to talk to you," she says.

"Uh huh," I respond, gritting my teeth.

"So, I think I want to be like a doctor or something."

"Like a doctor or something, got it."

"No! It needs to sound better. Here, let me see."

Emily puts her hand on mine for a second and I almost jump. Her skin is perfectly soft under her white school sweater. She takes the pen out of my hand and starts writing.

"You have to make me sound smart, OK?" she says.

"Sure," I say, laughing. *This is actually going so much better than I could have imagined.*

"Rosie!" I hear a familiar voice call in the distance. I'm so lost in the moment that I don't recognize who it is.

Then I see him. It's Jimmy. He's waving at me.

"Who's that?" Emily asks.

"I think he's in special ed," I hear one of the girls say, starting to giggle.

"Don't laugh at him!" I say. "He's just … my neighbor."

"Hey, Rosie," he says, walking up and still waving. He completely ignores Emily and stares straight at me. "I saw one!"

"Saw what?" I ask, meekly.

"One of the shadow people you told me about. Back at the apartment …"

"Jimmy! OK, we'll talk about it later, OK?" I say, talking over him.

"Wait a minute — I know you!" Emily says. "At Halloween, I think you came to my door dressed like a skeleton."

"That was me!" Jimmy says, excitedly.

"And you — was that you?"

"Ohhh shoot, I have to go actually," I say, grabbing my notebook and pen out of Emily's hand.

"Ow!" she says.

"Sorry!" I practically shout in her face as I drop the pen onto the grass. I reach down and pick it up, my fingers digging into the muddy ground, before stuffing my belongings back into my monstrous backpack. I run away but try to make it look like I'm walking by not moving my arms, making myself look even more awkward in the process. "We can finish later! In Spanish!" I call out to Emily, who replies, "Fine," or at least I think so.

Her friends watch me, bewildered, as Jimmy tries his best to catch up to me. But I'm not having it. I turn the corner and duck into the girl's bathroom, where I sit on the toilet for the last few minutes of break, cleaning my fingertips with toilet paper.

"Well that was really SUPER COOL!" I shout out into the bathroom. I hear giggling from the stall next to me, but I could care less at this point. This day couldn't get any worse.

It doesn't even occur to me until later what Jimmy said.

CHAPTER 26

On an otherwise boring Friday night, I'm trying to channel the Shadow Girl again. Since that last time, when she took me to the *other place*, she hasn't been back.

But the Shadow Man has. He's been visiting me, sometimes appearing for just a second before I fall asleep. Or after. It's hard to remember, and I feel powerless to do anything about it anyway. I know that the Shadow Girl tried to warn me about him, but ... I didn't listen.

The thing is, I'm really tired. It's funny — most nights I want to go to bed right away, then something strange happens, and the rest of the night is ruined. I wake up exhausted. This time, I want to stay up till Dad is good and asleep before I sneak out and try to summon the Shadow Girl in apartment 301.

I'm struggling. I pinch my own arm several times to stay awake. I blast my Nine Inch Nails cassingle until Dad comes in and tells me, "I thought I told you to throw that away!" He never actually checks that I do, so I keep it. I think it's not the parental advisory sticker on the cover of the tape that bothers him as much as the actual sound of it — menacing, harsh, evil. They really annoy him. I love Nine Inch Nails.

Anyway, Dad's still puttering around out there. I keep closing my door and opening it softly, pretending to get water or go to the bathroom. Dad notices, too. "Why do you keep getting up like that?" he asks me at one point. He's scribbling something on a notepad while sitting on the bed. He looks extra frazzled.

"I'm ... just thirsty," I tell him.

He closes the door on me without saying anything. I decide to give up, but after a few minutes, the light goes out in his room. *I guess he gave up on whatever he was doing.*

What's he gonna do, anyway? What's he gonna say? Nothing.

So I walk outside once I know he's not going to come out of his room again. The spring air feels cool on my skin. I pull my No Fear shirt (the one Aunt Rita got me but I'm too embarrassed to wear to school) to cover more of my arms and turn toward apartment 301.

Standing in front of it, I'm frozen again. *OK, Rosie, you've done this before. You know what you have to do.*

It's about midnight, the right time to make her appear. I reach town and turn the doorknob, and this time it turns.

I close the door behind me. There's an odd smell in the apartment. Before, it just smelled like new paint. Now, it's like something is rotting.

I walk around in my fuzzy slippers, waiting for my eyes to adjust. When they do, I sit cross-legged on the floor. *It's just the same as before,* I tell myself.

I close my eyes as if I were praying. *Mom would like that,* I think. She used to take me to Catholic Mass every Sunday — or at least every other Sunday. We only stopped once she was too sick to go.

I'm getting distracted, so instead, I start to picture the Shadow Girl coming out of the bedroom, peering around the corner just like she did before, thinking I can manifest her somehow. *I'll explain to her that I was just scared before, but I miss talking to her. I miss how she felt worried about me and tried to help me, even if she didn't always know how to do it right. She was trying. That's better than—*

My thoughts are interrupted by the sound of the bedroom door handle jiggling. I feel the familiar warmth. *She's here*, I think. I'm too excited to wait. I walk up to the bedroom door and try to open it.

Upon touching the handle, searing pain goes shooting through my hand. I scream and back up onto the floor, clutching my throbbing hand. The door flings open and The Shadow Man emerges. He stands before me, his strange head pulsating, his neck growing until he's as tall as the ceiling. He looks down at me with his hollow eyes. I can hear his voice in my head.

"You came back. And now you'll be with me forever."

"No!" I scream back.

He laughs. Shrill and high, it's like laughter just barely covering an awful shriek.

I pull myself up and run toward the front door. *Don't look back*, I think. *Last time, at school, you looked back. That's how he got to you. That's how he got in your head.* I want to look back so badly. But through my tears, I manage to pry open the door and shut it behind me. I can still hear his laughter echoing in my head.

It's still echoing. Even as I find myself back in bed. Clutching my hand. I'm awake now and it's burned. Now I remember his words. "You'll be with me forever."

CHAPTER 27

A few days later, it's my birthday. To my surprise, Dad remembers. It's just not necessarily the way I'd want him to.

We're in the car on the way to school when he finally mentions it.

"Thirteen. Big time!" he says, patting my back like I just threw a touchdown or something.

"Yeah," I say. "Look at me go."

"Oh honey," he says. "Must you always be so negative?"

"It's my birthday," I respond.

"That's true," he says. "You be however you want."

"Thanks, Dad."

"I was thinking," he begins. "You, me and Alison could go out for dinner and a movie tonight. What do you say?"

"Well," I say. "How can I say no?"

"That's my girl," he says, somehow missing the sarcasm dripping from my voice entirely.

"I guess it'll be better than the average Wednesday. It has to be," I mutter, reaching my hand out in front of me. The burn still stings.

"Is your hand OK?" Dad asks without looking at me. I don't answer him.

*

At lunch, Jane ribs me. "I can't believe you didn't tell us it was your birthday!"

"I only knew because Señora Chang said so and made her wear the birthday sombrero all through class," Alex says.

"Yeah, that was a real treat," I say. "Muy bueno."

"Rosie! Happy birthday!" Alex says cheerily, hugging me. I'm thrilled, obviously, and I look over at Jane, who doesn't push her glasses up and look away this time.

"What should we do?" Jane asks.

"Um, well it's today," I say. "Dad's supposed to take me to dinner with Alison."

"So he's using your birthday to bring his girlfriend around? That bites."

"We gotta do something," Alex says. "Why don't we all go to your place Friday?"

A feeling of dread washes over me. Our building is weird enough for me on a daily basis. The thought of Alex being there is mortifying. But it also kind of excites me.

"Alex! You can't just invite yourself to people's houses," Jane says.

"It's not a house, it's just an old apartment building." As I say it, my living situation starts to feel like a nuisance to me. *I'm not gonna let that crap get in the way.*

"Let's do it," I say.

"Will your dad mind if I come?" Alex says.

"Nah, he doesn't care about anything I do," I say. Jane and Alex both stay quiet. "I mean, he'll probably just hang around and watch 'Cheers' in his room or something lame."

"Wait, Rosie, didn't you say your place was haunted?" Jane says with a mouthful of fries.

"What?" Alex says. "You never told me about that!" Alex is a huge horror movie fan like me, and I knew he'd love this. But I was, of course, too shy and embarrassed to share any of this information with him.

"Yeah," I say, acting as nonchalant as I can. "It kind of is."

"How?"

"We'll find out," Jane says, winking at Alex. I don't know what she means, but I'm excited, particularly because whatever they have in store for me sounds way better than dinner with Dad and Alison tonight.

After school, Dad rolls up to pick me up with Alison already in the car. He's wearing a leather jacket I've never seen before, and the Chevy gleams red with a fresh wash.

"Hi honey!" he says, rolling down the window.

"Hey Rose," Alison says from behind a pair of circular, John Lennon sunglasses in the passenger seat.

"It's Rosie," I say. "You don't have work or something?"

"Nope. Took the night off," she says, jabbing Dad playfully. I'm not sure she means by this —maybe she doesn't work.

"Are you ready for your big night, birthday girl?" Dad says, as I get into the car and slam the door behind me.

"I have homework," I say.

"You do?"

"Yeah, it's this whole school thing, Dad."

"Oh honey," Dad says. "We'll just make something up for you."

"Dad," I say. "It's too early anyway. I just ate."

"OK, OK," he says, turning toward home. "We'll head home first."

Back in the apartment, I try to get through Spanish homework at the counter while Alison sits on the couch, drinking a glass of milk. *So weird. What adult drinks a glass of milk?* Alison has ditched the young mom look from before. Today, her Rachel cut has been styled into a platinum-blonde Marilyn Monroe look, which makes her appear a little bit older but is still an improvement. She wears tight, faded jeans and a denim jacket over a white T-shirt with Chinese characters swiped across it. Underneath the characters, it reads, "GIRLS KICK ASS," and a foot doing a karate kick.

"It's a really cool apartment," she says, pressing her long fingers into the couch. "I heard you have your own room."

"Yeah," I say.

"Can I see it?"

"Go ahead."

"Honey," Dad says, cutting in from the kitchen. "Why don't you show Alison your room?"

"Dad, I have a lot of Spanish work to do."

"Honey."

"OK," I say, getting up. "Right this way."

I lead her down the hall and open the door to my room, flipping on the switch. My bed's unmade, and I have a sketchpad out.

"Sorry it's messy," I say. "I didn't know anyone was coming over."

"It's OK. I heard you like music," she says, pointing to my Nirvana poster.

"Yeah," I say.

"Nirvana," she says. "Coo-ool."

"Yup," I say. "They're great."

"Have you ever been to any shows?" she asks. "Last week I saw the Spin Doctors, and I got to go backstage! My dad knows their manager. They even said my name on stage! Isn't that cool?"

I snort. Alison's smile fades. "Sorry," I say. "I had something in my throat. That's really cool! I have to finish my homework real fast."

I run back to the kitchen counter, but it's pointless. Dad and Alison chat between the kitchen and the couch as if I'm not there, lobbing useless comments about "the biz" to one another like, "What's a treatment, exactly?" and "How many revisions is normal?" I finally put down my *pluma*, leaving my homework unfinished.

"I think that I know Spanish now," I say. "I'm ready to go."

"Where do you wanna go, honey?" Dad asks. I really want Chinese food. I look over at Alison and her stupid shirt. "How about Italian?"

We go to the Cheesecake Factory, and I try to make nice while Alison talks about all the famous people her dad knows. I can't figure out how old she is — something like a 32-year-old with the boobs of an 18-year-old and the mind of a 7-year-old.

Alison taps the menu with her bright red nails. *She's actually pretty*, I think. *Just sort of embarrassing.*

"What's tetrazzini?" she asks, wrinkling her nose.

"Where's the waiter? What's taking so long?" Dad says, fidgeting with his jacket zipper. He gets up to find someone, and I wonder why he's so tense.

Alison leans over to me. "So, have you read any of your dad's stuff?" she asks.

"No, he doesn't let me," I say, smiling and thinking about the time Jessica and I sneaked a peek.

"Well, it's probably because it's a little mature for you. He's really good," she says, smiling. "When you're older, you'll appreciate it. Maybe you'll even see it on the big screen one day." She winks at me.

"Oh. Can't wait," I say, swinging my arm and giving a thumbs up in mock excitement.

We eat in relative silence. I push my meatballs around my plate and deliberately make scratching noises with my fork.

When Alison goes to the bathroom, Dad asks, "So, honey, what do you think of Alison?"

"Well, she's …"

"Honey, I know she's not the brightest girl. She's nothing like you and nothing like your mother. But different people have different things to offer. And Alison is a good person with a good heart. I think she's going to be great for me and could be a great stepmom to you too, someday. I'm sorry, honey, if you don't like her yet, but you have to give things time. And I know things have been tough in school and everything, but you have to at least try. Could you do that for me, honey?" He clasps my shoulder tightly.

"Ow, Dad. I was just gonna say she's nice."

"Oh shit, he didn't get you a present, did he?" Alison says, returning with a nail file.

"I have to go to the bathroom," I say, running away.

I'm taking my time to wash my hands in the bathroom to avoid going back to them. "Well this is easily the worst birthday ever," I say to myself in the mirror.

My thoughts drift back to my seventh birthday. *That was on my birthday, that memory of Karen and I being best friends and swinging all day. That was all I needed to feel happy then. Poor Karen.*

"Karen," I say, staring into the mirror. The realization hits me like a truck. "It's Karen."

Karen is dead. Every time I've been to the room when the Shadow Girl came, I had her with me. Or when she visited me in my room, the doll was there. When I didn't have her with me, that's when he came ...

I have to go back. Even if he comes again ... there's only one way to know.

"Dad, I wanna leave," I say when I come back.

"What about the movies? I thought we were gonna see 'Outbreak.'"

"I'm ... not feeling well. Too much tetrazzini."

"Oh, gotcha. OK! We just have to take Alison home first."

We wrap up our blah pastas drive 20 minutes to a white-pillared estate with an endless lawn in Beverly Hills. It feels worlds away from our crappy apartment in North Hollywood.

"Bye, Rosie!" she says. "Cool birthday."

"Cool," I say, waving back to her.

On the way home, I kick the backseat. "Dad," I say.

"Yes, honey?"

"For my birthday present, I want a real birthday. I want my friends to come over Friday and have pizza. OK?"

"Sure, honey. It's your day," he says, sighing.

*

When we get home, Dad immediately jumps on the phone.

"Dad …" I say. "Who are you talking to?"

"Huh? Just Alison, sweetie."

"Already? You just saw her."

"What is it, honey?"

"I'm gonna go say hi to Jimmy."

"It's getting late."

"It'll just be a minute. You won't even notice me come back in."

"Sure, honey."

With that, I knock on Jimmy's door. He's already in his pajamas, but I tell Vera it's important. When she's in the kitchen, I tell Jimmy, "hey, Jimmy, you remember Karen? My doll?"

"She's my doll now," he says.

"Yeah, she's yours," I reply. "But … is it OK if borrow her?"

"You gave her to me!" he says.

"I know, but … it's my birthday."

"No!"

"Jimmy!" Vera says, coming in from the other room. "You have to give her the doll back. It's very important to her. It was a gift from her mother."

Jimmy whimpers and runs off to his room. I can't meet Vera's eye. What would I say to her? How could I explain myself?

Luckily, I don't have to. "I understand, lovey," she says. "You were trying to do something nice. But you shouldn't give something so important away."

"Yeah," I say, still staring down. "I'm sorry about it. It's just … with my birthday …" I don't know what else to say without feeling foolish.

"You don't have to explain it to me, dear."

Jimmy returns with the doll. I take it with only slight hesitation from Jimmy. "I'll bring it back," I say.

"You don't have to. I don't want it!" With that, Jimmy storms off to his room. I mutter a quick goodbye to Vera and leave the apartment.

Once outside, I realize how irrational I'm being. *That was really mean of me,* I think. *And for what? To see if this … thing you might be imagining shows up?'*

I look down at my hand. The white blister in the middle of my palm sits there as proof. *I'm not crazy. And Jimmy will be fine.*

I determinedly enter apartment 301. Setting Karen down in front of me, I take my place on the carpet and sit. I wait. I do my trick, closing my eyes for a few moments and opening them again, hoping time will have magically passed. Every time I open them, fear shoots through me. Fear that I'm wrong. That it will be him standing there. He'll do something awful to me. Maybe this birthday will be my last.

I close my eyes again. I hear a soft voice.

"Happy birthday," it whispers. I open my eyes and she's there. The Shadow Girl.

"You remembered," I say.

"Of course I did."

I'm so happy that I start crying.

"What's wrong?" she says. She looks down. "I'm so sorry. About the last time. You should run away and never come back. Maybe you're better off …"

"No," I say. "It's OK. I just … I need to be careful. But … I figured it out. I figured out who you are."

The Shadow Girl says nothing. I point to the doll. "You're … her, aren't you? Karen." She stands silently, the dark strands of hair flowing around her face.

Finally, she speaks. "OK. I am Karen."

"Karen," I say. "I'm so happy. I wish I could hug you!"

"I wish I could, too," she says.

I sit up with her half the night. She asks me how I'm doing, how my birthday was, whispering words of encouragement to me. When sleep once again comes naturally to me, I wind up back in bed. *You saved my birthday, Karen.*

CHAPTER 28

Dad agrees to let me have Alex and Jane over. It doesn't seem to register to him that Alex is a guy and that that's kind of a big deal. Dad says he'll be there, though, which is surprising because Fridays are usually his night to go out wherever he goes and leave me at Vera and Jimmy's.

On Friday, Alex and Jane take the bus home with me. I sneak into the seat with Alex first, and Jane sits in front of us, turning around to talk to us.

"I'm excited to see where you live," Alex says.

"Oh, it's kind of crappy," I say.

"It can't be much worse than my house."

"Alex, did you bring the goods?" Jane asks.

"I sure did. It's in my backpack."

"What is?" I ask.

"It's a surprise, stupid," Jane says. "It's your birthday present."

"Sit down back there!" calls out the bus driver, a large, crotchety white woman with a mullet.

"Oh, bite me," Jane whispers, sitting back down.

We get up to the apartment, throw our bags down on the couch and grab Cokes from the fridge. I look around the place and realize how bare the walls are. Dad and I clean a bit on weekends, but it still looks a little grimy, the walls having faded from white to eggshell. *This place really is a dump,* I think. *Oh well ... too late.*

I go looking for Dad, but he isn't home.

"Nice place," Alex says.

"My Dad isn't home," I say nervously.

"Can we see your room?" Jane asks.

I show them into my room, which is pretty messy, but with these two, I don't care. Alex flops onto my bed and looks at the shelf of tapes above my headboard. Jane starts looking at my desk while I open the window blinds.

"What are these?" Jane asks. Given how scatterbrained I've been lately, I've forgotten to put away my drawings. I don't mind though, really. Jane thumbs through sketches I've done of the apartment, of Jimmy, Vera and Dad. Then she gets to the last few. The Shadow Girl staring ahead, glowing lines surrounding her silhouette.

"These are really cool," she says. "What are they?"

"Oh," I say. I hesitate. "That's ..."

"Are these the ghosts?" Alex says, getting up.

"Yeah, something like that," I say with a nervous laugh.

"Wow," Alex says, mesmerized, staring at my simple sketch of the Shadow Man. Truthfully, I don't remember doing that one. And I don't like seeing it now. *He's gone now,* I think. *It's OK.*

"We should probably leave for a bit," I say. "My dad's not here. I'm not sure if he'll get mad ..."

"Oh, duh," Jane says, motioning to Alex to get out of the room.

We leave and walk over to the construction site, because there isn't anything else around worth doing. To my surprise, they love it.

"This is so cool," Jane says, poking around the lonely wooden frames of the would-be shops. "This is perfect."

"For what?" I ask.

"You'll see."

Alex spins around a metal pole sticking out of the ground. He seems distracted. He looks graceful, spinning on one foot. It occurs to me how little he cares about the way he looks, or whether he's macho enough, hanging out with two girls like this. I love him for that.

"I'd rather live here than my house," he says.

"Where, in this pile of dirt?" Jane asks.

"No, just … over here. Away from my mom and dad."

"Do you see your dad a lot?" I ask him.

"No. We don't really get along."

"Oh, sorry. My dad's weird, too."

"I'll take weird any day over—"

Alex stops talking as a long black town car drives up into the parking lot in front. The window rolls down, and a stern man in a gray suit wearing sunglasses looks us up and down from inside the car. His look is familiar to me, but I can't put my finger on why.

"You're not supposed to be here," he tells us. He motions for us to leave with his hand. I try to look into the back seat, but all I see is the shadowy outline of a person.

"Hey, no problem, we'll get outta here," Alex says. He takes me by the arm, and we walk back toward my apartment. I look back and see the man's head hanging out of the window as he stares us down.

Jane catches up. "We'll just have to make do in your place," she says.

We go back in through the parking garage, and I see Dad's car parked in its spot. We walk up the stairs, and I quickly point to Mr. Ennis' door.

"This is what I was talking about," I whisper in Alex's ear. He holds his mouth to keep from laughing, and we scramble up the stairs. When we're almost in, I hear a door open behind me.

"Hey, Rosie!" I hear Jimmy say. "Who are they?"

"Oh, hey Jimmy," I say. "These are some friends of mine."

"Are you guys having a party?"

"No, we're just … doing homework," I say.

"But it's Friday."

"I know. Big project. I'll see you later, OK, Jimmy?"

He frowns and holds onto the door handle, and I motion for Jane and Alex to enter as I open the door. "Sorry, that's my neighbor. He's kind of weird," I say, instantly feeling bad about it. That feeling is soon replaced by horror; Dad's here with Alison.

"Hi honey!" Dad says cheerily. "Who are all your friends?"

I make quick introductions and give Dad my best death stare.

"Pizza's on its way, and we rented a couple movies," Dad says. VHS copies of *Jurassic Park* and *Dead Again* sit on our scratched glass coffee table.

"We'll leave you kids alone," Alison says, indicating Dad's bedroom. I feel rage boiling up inside me that he brought Alison when my friends were here, but it subsides. *At least they'll be out of our hair.*

Once we've eaten and Dad and Alison are away, we pop in *Jurassic Park*, but our interest soon vanishes. Jane unzips her backpack and pulls out a long, thin game box. She flips it over to reveal a Oujia board.

"Merry Christmas!" she says.

I'm so touched by the fact that they got me something that I don't stop to think about what the thing is actually for.

"We were thinking we might try to use it over at that construction site," Alex says. "But we'll have to settle for your living room."

"C'mon," Jane says. "Let's find out if this place is haunted for reals. Maybe your shadow people will show up."

We move the pizza box aside and unfold the Ouija board. A dinosaur roars in the background. Jane grabs the remote and hits mute.

"Not here on the couch," Jane says. She motions over to an area of the carpet toward the window. Alex goes to the front door to flip the light switch. There's intensity in his hazel eyes as he looks at me, asking silently if this is OK. I look toward the hallway and hear Alison laughing. I nod.

We sit in a circle around the board and put our fingers down. "Now, Rosie, what do you want to ask?" Jane says.

I sit for a minute with my eyes closed. I can see the visions in my mind playing back like a video tape. "I want to know ... who they are."

"Who is visiting Rosie?" Alex asks.

Our fingers start to move with the plastic game piece. The lens in the piece crosses over letter by letter without stopping. It finally skids to "I" and stops. It moves over to "A," then "M." It stops, then starts again, scooting slowly to "H," then "E," "R" and finally "E."

"I am here," Alex says.

"Good one," Jane says.

"I didn't do anything!" Alex says, laughing. "I woulda done something funnier than that."

I don't say anything. I don't know how serious to take this, or how serious Alex and Jane are taking it.

"OK, whatever," Jane says. "So, 'I,' what do you want?"

Nothing happens for a bit. Then the plastic piece begins to slide again, moving over to "R," then "O." It slides over to "S," and Jane scoffs.

"OK, Alex, we know that you want Rosie," Jane says.

"I told you I'm not moving it!" Alex says.

I'm distracted by Alex's blushing and the closeness of his fingers to mine. I don't notice the piece finishing out my name until it stops on "E."
"Well, what do you want from Rosie, hmm?" Jane asks. "You want to ask her to the spring dance?"

The piece starts to move more violently.

"Hey, chill out," Jane says.

The piece moves to "D."

"How many times do I have to tell you, I'm not doing anything?" Alex says.

It moves to "E." Then "D." It stops.

"What? Is it done?" Jane asks.

"What did it say?" Alex asks.

"It wants me dead," I say.

I look over at Jane and see a dark, oblong head looming over her, with black arms outstretched toward me. The shock sends a bolt of adrenaline through me, my breath coming out in short fast bursts until I start screaming and fall backwards.

"Hey! Are you OK?" Alex asks, grabbing onto me.

The bedroom door bursts open. Dad comes out, adjusting his shirt. "Rosie!" he says. "What are you guys doing?"

Alison follows behind him. "Oh relax, they're just playing spin the bottle!" she says, giggling.

"OK, party's over," Dad says. I look over at a confused Jane. My eyes flash toward the glowing blue light of the TV behind her, where a T-Rex roars silently, his little arms outstretched. *Was that all I saw? The dumb dinosaur from Jurassic Park on the TV? But it seemed so real.*

Dad flips on the lights and stomps around the apartment picking up our cups of soda and paper plates full of pizza grease. Alex sits quietly for a moment before asking if he can use the phone to call his mom. *Is Alex as freaked out as I am? No, he probably just feels awkward and wants to leave. I don't blame him. But, if the Shadow Man is back, I can't be alone with just Dad tonight.*

I grab onto Jane's sweater sleeve. "Dad," I say.

"What?" he answers.

"Can Jane stay over? Please?"

"Sure," he says with a huff.

CHAPTER 29

It's the week after my birthday, and I'm completely frazzled.

I'm still not sleeping much at all. I haven't been back to apartment 301. I'm just ... not ready yet.

At night, I toss and turn, thinking about the Shadow Man, and I clutch Karen to me for protection. *Was the Ouija board stuff just Alex or Jane playing a mean joke and my mind playing tricks on me? Alex would never do that*, I think. *Jane, maybe.*

But they both confirm to me at lunch one day that it wasn't either of them who did it. "Why the hell would I do that?" is what Jane actually says. "That's messed up."

"Don't look at me," Alex says.

"Well, what was it then?" I ask, exasperated.

"Calm down," Jane says. "I mean, it spelled D-E-D. Your ghost can't even spell. Maybe it was her," she says, bobbing her head toward Nora Nagy, who sits by herself eating some chowder-like substance from a glassware container. Not only is Nora actively disliked, she's almost failing English, probably on account of it being her second language. She's lodged herself in a hardly visible area between a pole and the vending machines. *Good idea, Nora*, I think to myself. *That's what I would've done before; it's about the least visible place you could find.*

"Be nice to Nora," I say, after staring at her a moment. "She's weird, but I feel bad for her."

"Sorr-ee," Jane says, dramatically.

I leave them and approach Nora. Jane's annoying me with her constant rudeness. I was just like Nora, once.

When I reach her, I realize I don't really know what I'm going to say. So, I just say, "Hey, Nora."

Nora looks up from her gruel, but she doesn't reply.

"Uh ... how's it going?" I offer.

"Shouldn't you be with your friends," she says, rather than asks. She looks back down at her food.

"Um, yeah, no, it's OK, I'll go back to them later. I wanted to see what you were up to."

"Eating," she says.

"Oh. That's cool ..."

"You don't have to talk to me."

"No, I want to."

"No, you don't. You just feel bad for me. You have friends now. You used to have no friends."

"That's not true!" I say. I'm not really convinced, though. I'm surprised by how well Nora can see right through me.

"Well," I say finally. "Maybe you're right."

I feel like this might be a step toward getting to know Nora better, that she would like it that I agreed with her. But instead, she just glowers at me. Her blonde locks don't hide her blue eyes that look like they could cut through stone right now, although she seems less mean when I realize her lunch goop has stained the overalls she seems to wear every day.

"I didn't mean anything by that," I say.

"Just leave me alone!" she says, getting up. "You think you're different, but … you're just the same!" I can tell she wants to cry. I don't know what to say now, so I don't say anything. She starts to walk away but then turns around. "You know, you want everyone to like you. That's why they hate you."

"People don't hate me!" I say indignantly.

"*He* does," she says, her blue eyes radiating with intensity. *Where have I seen eyes like that before?*

The Shadow Boy. His piercing blue eyes. Could she be ….?

Nora walks away without saying anything else. I return to Jane and Alex.

"What did you say to her?" Jane says, stifling a laugh.

"Nothing! I hardly said anything. And she was so mean to me. What's … what's her freaking problem?"

"Dang, I've never seen Rosie so pissed!" Alex says.

"She said 'he hates me,'" I say.

"Oh, she would say something like that. She had a big crush on Alex. Nora used to have one friend, Tatiana, and she made Tatiana ask Alex if he liked Nora. He was like, 'No way!'" she says, deepening her voice to mimic Alex's.

"Shut up, Jane! I didn't know she was gonna tell her that."

"Maybe …" Jane says thoughtfully. "Maybe she put a curse on you."

"What?" I ask.

"Well, you said your place was haunted. Then we saw what happened with the Ouija board. It's possible. You know she's like a gypsy or whatever."

"That's racist!" Alex says. "Maybe you cast a Korean spell on her."

"I'm gonna Korean kick your ass if you don't shut the hell up,"

Jane says.

I stop paying attention to what they're saying. *Is it possible that Nora has some sort of mystical power, so she can see my weird dreams and visions? No, that's impossible. She was just talking about Alex, right? It must be so obvious that I like him.*

"I don't hate you, obviously," Alex says, touching my arm and shaking me out of my stupor.

"What?" I say.

"Alex, you'll make the birthday girl blush," Jane says in a mock motherly tone. "Don't get her all hot and bothered before the midterm."

I hit Jane's arm, and she hits mine back.

"Ow!" she says.

"You deserve it!"

It's playful, but I realize I hit Jane harder than I meant to. She looks genuinely annoyed for a moment, but I'm too lost in my thoughts to let it bother me. Before anyone else can say another word, the bell rings.

CHAPTER 30

The bus careens down Wilshire Boulevard, past old-looking buildings and scattered homeless people. As the bus hits potholes, Alex and I bump into each other awkwardly, laughing and holding onto the seat in front of us.

School is holding two days of field trips to the La Brea Tar Pits, and Alex and I are in the first group. Jane is going tomorrow, so it's just the two of us today.

It's the first time Alex and I have spent a lot of time together alone. At school, he and Jane have practically every class together, except for Spanish, which is just me and him. Jane's parents wouldn't let her miss school even if she was dying, so they're almost always together.

I've been sleeping so badly lately, and once I learned the field trip was just going to be the two of us, the excitement has only made it worse. *What am I going to wear? Will we be able to sit together?*

The answer to the second question is yes. The first: a Doors T-shirt, my favorite worn-in Levi's and my imitation Docs from Target. Alex said I looked cool in this outfit once, so it was kind of a no-brainer.

"Who are the Doors?" Alex asks me on the bus.

"You don't know who the Doors are?" I ask incredulously.

"No. Do they have a new CD out?"

"No, they're dead. Or Jim Morrison is."

"Is he—"

"The singer. Him," I say, pointing to his sullen face on my T-shirt.

"Oh," Alex says, staring at it a moment. "He looks bummed out."

"He was, I guess," I say. I take out my Walkman and stretch the metal band of the headphones as far as they'll go. "Here, listen. I think you'll like it."

We put our heads close together and listen to "People Are Strange." Alex starts to laugh at it, and I look at him in annoyance. "I like it," he mouths to me, and I smile.

"No music!" I hear shouted through my headphones from the front of the bus. It's crotchety mullet lady again.

"Who cares?" I say, stuffing the headphones into my backpack. "It's just headphones."

"She's strange," he says. "People are strange—"

"Oh my God, don't sing!" I scream.

"Be quiet back there!" shouts the crotchety woman.

When we get off the bus, we're practically holding hands as we learn about all the prehistoric animals that got stuck in the tar pits. Alex keeps naming them.

"That one's Bobby," he says, pointing to a bobcat. "That one looks like Emily, right?" he says, pointing to a huge mammoth. "That one's named Mrs. Sailor," he says, pointing to a hyena with a wide grin like our teacher's. I hit his arm and try to stifle laughs while the docent talks over us.

So far, it's been one of the best days of my life.

We reach a gated area where a fake wooly mammoth stands in a dark pool. As the docent talks about the poor mammoth's fate, Alex takes pictures of us and of the exhibit — he has permission because of yearbook. Mr. Minogle and the others start to move on to the next exhibit, but Alex tells me to stop.

"I wanna take a better picture of you, close up," he says.

"Oh, OK, sure," I say, smirking.

"Don't smile though," he says.

"Fine, I'll try," I say.

"There. You look tough."

"Thanks," I say. I try to act cool, but I start to giggle as he tells me, "You're a star."

"All right, that's enough," I say.

Alex has moved on to taking more pictures of the surroundings, and I'm just kind of waiting for him, making sure we're not so far away from the others as to get in trouble. I'm not sure what to do with myself, so I ask him, "Why do you like taking pictures?"

He doesn't answer me for a minute and keeps snapping. "It's fun," he says. Then, after a pause, "I started taking them a lot when my parents split up. It's pretty boring when it's just two of us. My mom got me this camera the Christmas right after it happened, probably because she felt bad or something."

"Sorry," I say. "I kind of did the same thing with my Mom, when she died. I started drawing a lot more. The shrink told me to do something to take my mind off of it."

"Well," he says, "you're really good at it."

"Thanks," I reply. "So are you."

Alex seems so far away all of a sudden. He's stopped taking pictures and is just staring at the mammoth.

"It's so sad," he says finally.

I'm unsure how to respond. "Yeah."

"They couldn't do anything about it. Just had to sit there and die."

"Jeez. You're depressing."

"It's true, though. Something like that could happen now and we couldn't do nothing about it," he says, coming closer to me. My heart is practically beating out of my chest.

"Well, we're not dead yet," I say. I mean it to sound cheery, but it sounds dark. I look at Alex, and he's not smiling anymore.

"Remember the Ouija board?" he asks.

We'd been having such a good time that I almost forgotten about that. "Yeah," I say.

"My dad said something like ... what is said to you, once," he says. "He said it would be better if I was dead."

"Oh my God," I whisper. "Alex, that's ... so terrible."

"Yeah," Alex says, looking away. I think he may be crying, but I try not to look, to give him space. Within a few seconds, he turns and runs after Mr. Minogle and the other kids. "C'mon, we're getting left behind."

I follow a few steps behind him. For the rest of the day, we're both pretty quiet. I'm struck by the suddenness of his comment, but also happy, in a way, that he felt like he could tell me something like that. *Maybe I could tell him more about ... no, that's not a good idea. He's maybe just starting to like me. I don't want him to think I'm crazy.*

Back in the museum, we're waiting quietly in line to get back on the bus next to another line of students about our age. They're in Catholic school uniforms, a row of girls chatting away. *I wish I had more girlfriends,* I think. I notice that they're all white, with blonde or brown hair, like me. Like all my friends back home. *At least here, everyone doesn't look the same.*

Even as I notice how similar they look, one of them at them stands out to me. She has short, brown hair, and she's talking rapidly to another girl, as if she were trying to get all of her words out before they vanished from her mind.

I must be staring a while because her friend nudges her and she turns to look at me. Even though it's been years, I realize who she is right away: It's Karen.

I walk over to her slowly, our eyes locked. She gives me no sign of recognition. I'm staring at her straight in the eye, visions of our childhood flooding into my brain.

"Karen," I say. "Is it really you?"

"Aubrey?" she asks. "Is … that really you?"

"I can't believe it!" I say, and we hug, laughing. "You're alive! You're here and you're real!"

We only have seconds to catch up. She and her family are doing well; they moved to California and settled in Orange County. She takes out a marker and writes her number on my hand before her class is whisked away.

My head is spinning when I return to Alex. "What was *that* all about?" he asks.

"You won't believe it."

I fill Alex in as we enter the bus. I'm giddy as I recount to him how I thought she had passed away, but that she had survived at least long enough for me to see her again. I jot her number down in my sketch pad before it washes off and vow to call her the next day.

As the bus cruises back toward school, I start to think about what his means. *The Shadow Girl isn't Karen because Karen is alive. I guess she was just playing along to make me feel better.*

I shake myself out of it when I realize Alex has been almost completely quiet the whole time — and he's *never* quiet.

"Hey — are you OK?" I finally ask.

"Yeah, I'm fine," he says, but he doesn't look at me.

I pull out my Walkman again without saying anything else, and we hunch down in our seats so Mullet Lady can't see us. I slip the foam headphone over his ear and put the other over mine. "The End" by The Doors plays. It's a long song, and we listen to its sullen military march as we watch the sun illuminate old theaters and signs in Korean. My hand creeps toward his, but I stop short of touching it, waiting for him to make a move. He doesn't.

But I do — kind of. After all the excitement of the day, I'm so tired that I can't keep my head up. I lay my head on his, and he doesn't flinch. He doesn't really respond to it, either, but at least he lets my head rest there.

I let my eyes close, and I think about those fossils at the museum — how long they've been around and all the things that have happened while they've been sitting there, watching. Mom would've loved it. We used to go to the Art Institute of Chicago together and loved looking at all the old Egyptian stuff, the sarcophaguses and ankhs and all that. I think we both felt more at home there than anywhere else.

I'm picturing her sitting next to me now. Leaning on Alex's shoulder reminds me of falling asleep on Mom's lap during long road trips, when she'd sit in the back seat with me. Stroking my hair. I run my hand through my own hair, but the headphones are in the way. Some of my hair is stuck in it, so I open my eyes to pull it out before it gets worse and I make an ass of myself.

But Alex is gone. So is everyone. It's nighttime now. *Is it possible they all left me here? How could Alex have done that?*

I look out the window, expecting to see the school parking lot, but I don't recognize where I am. I move toward the front of the bus, but I'm not sure how to open the door. I finally find a way to push it open and I walk outside.

I'm still at the museum. How is this possible? It's pitch black and cold. I think about all the rundown storefronts we saw on the way here and realize I shouldn't be standing out here alone.

I run toward the museum building, shivering in my hoodie. I knock on the glass door, hoping to see a security guard, but it's no use. Maybe there's one around the corner? I run around the building and see the central lake pit Alex and I stood beside earlier that day. *Someone's moving there. It has to be a security guard.*

But what if it's not?

I can't stay here forever.

I walk toward the pit, trying my best to be inconspicuous. Looking around, I see that the parking lot is empty.

I reach the pit without seeing anyone. Instead, I see something bubbling up from the lake.

It takes me a minute to see what it is as it emerges from the tar. It's the skeleton of some long-dead dinosaur, one that stands on two legs and looks about the size of a man. But I realize the bones have no substance to them. It's just the suggestion of a dinosaur. There's nothing there but emptiness, a black space shaped like a skeleton with two gaping eye holes looking directly at me.

I turn to run, but then realize my feet are stuck in the mud. It gurgles, like the tar pit, enveloping my boots. I feel cool, black liquid touch my ankles, trickling upwards, up my legs as if I were hung upside-down.

"I ... can't move," I say. It feels like the tar has moved into my chest, filling my lungs. Hardly a sound comes out. Just spittle and breath.

The black head of the dinosaur lurches and stretches upward on a long, spindly neck. It curves and bends over the fence toward me in a giant arch. I stand immobile, waiting for it to do whatever it wants to me.

The head moves closer until it's breathing in my face. Cold, stale breath, like the breath that comes out of you during the worst Illinois winter.

Spit dribbles down my chin as I try to speak, but nothing comes out except a low breath.

"Rosie," it whispers.

I clear my throat as best as I can. "What ... do ... you ... want?"

"I want what's best for you," it says, its voice a high, warped lilt. "But you have to let me in."

"Let ... me ... go."

"You have to let yourself go, Rosie. You have to let me in."

The mud has seeped up my legs, past my knees. I can feel it hardening.

Let myself go?

"All right," I say. "OK."

The head lurches from side to side. "OK?"

"OK," I whisper.

"It's just a dream," I hear a voice say.

The voice is soothing. Warm breath on my neck.

My eyes scan from side to side. *The cars ... there are cars standing still in the middle of the road. That shouldn't be.*

"It's just a dream," I whisper hoarsely.

"It's just a dream," I repeat, clearing my throat.

The head leans in closer, resting on my shoulder. Despite its lack of substance, it's heavy, digging into me.

"Stop," I say.

The head lurches backward. "It's too late," it says.

Long, curling tendrils sprout from the back of its head.

"Why don't you just kiss him?" it says.

"What?"

My head moves forward and Alex's head, resting on top of mine, falls limp. My eyes snap open and I breathe heavily. I instinctively wipe the drool away from my mouth with the sleeve of my hoodie. The headphones snap off of our heads and I straighten up, hitting Alex in the ear.

"Ow," he says, rubbing his ear and straightening his neck.

"We're here. Time to wake up, lovebirds!" the bus driver says, looming over us with wide blue eyes, her mullet curling around her face like a mane. Everyone within earshot laughs at us. I turn beet-red. Alex, cool as always, just laughs.

"Thanks a lot," I say to her as I'm getting off the bus.

"I told you, no music!"

CHAPTER 31

That evening, I tell Dad about seeing Karen on the field trip, even though it was so brief and surreal that I can't be sure it even really happened. "It was so weird," I say as I eat my Yoshinoya chicken bowl. "She was just ... there!"

"Karen? From Galena?"

"Yes! Like, she seemed totally normal and healthy. I mean, I didn't really get to talk to her that much, but I'm going to call her right after school tomorrow. She doesn't live that far away."

"Well, what do you know?" Dad says, sort of vacantly.

"Yeah, it's pretty wild." *What's with him? Maybe Alison dumped him or something.*

Lying in bed, it feels like something has shifted within me since I saw that vision of the Shadow Man earlier. Instead of frightened, I feel ... alive. Like I let go of something I was holding onto. *Karen isn't the Shadow Girl because she's alive and there is no Shadow Girl. Well, no more quiet, meek little Rosie. No more imaginary friends. No more shadow people.*

The next morning, I run into Mr. N in the hallway before school. I fess up and hand him the key to apartment 301. I tell him that I kept it by accident. I don't want anything to do with that place anymore.

After school, in yearbook, I keep staring at Alex and thinking about how he seemed to be finding excuses to touch me on my birthday and during the field trip. He just bleached his hair again, and it looks so good against his tanned skin.

"Have you gotten any answers yet?" he asks me.

"Hmm?" I ask.

"For your yearbook project."

"Oh, just a few," I say. In reality, my humiliating attempt at interviewing Emily has been the beginning and end of my efforts so far. "Have you taken any new pictures lately?" I ask, changing the subject. "What about the ones from the tar pits?"

Everyone is working on their own projects, so Alex leads me into the darkroom without so much as a word to Señora Chang. She trusts us both. But I can feel my skin getting flushed. I've heard a lot of whispers about the darkroom being a place kids can get away with things Mrs. Sailor wouldn't allow on campus. *But nothing would happen with Alex ... would it?*

Why not? I think. It's a thought that doesn't even seem my own.

We start looking at a few prints hanging on a wire. There's one of Alex, with his fingers in his mouth and his tongue sticking out.

"You weren't supposed to see that one," he says sheepishly as I point and snicker. "That was just a test pic!"

"Sure, sure," I tease. "Some serious photographer you are."

He points to another photo and I see myself, staring at a wooly mammoth. It's a side profile shot, and I don't even look like myself. Or maybe I'm just not used to seeing myself from that angle. I've only recently gotten my hair cut, and I look kind of zoned out (as usual). *I look ... so much older than before.*

"You know that girl?" he asks.

"Hardly," I say. I get closer to the photo to look at the background. The lake stretches out behind me. *I can't make it out in this lighting, but it almost looks like there's something bubbling in the middle ...*

"Be careful," Alex says, startling me. "I like that one. Don't want to mess it up."

"Yeah, OK," I say, laughing and blushing a little.

I point to a shot of a group of girls standing on the front lawn of school, flashing peace signs. "Do you know these girls?" I ask.

"Oh yeah, that one's Marissa, I have her in Pre-Algebra with me."

"Oh, do you?" I ask. Alex laughs nervously. Looking at Marissa's smiling face, flowing hair and big, bright eyes, I suddenly feel like the photo of me I saw looks so ... sad, in comparison. "Do you think she's pretty?" I ask.

"Uh, she's OK," Alex says. He seems uncomfortable, looking down, his voice becoming quieter.

"Ugh," I say, dramatically. "She's friends with Emily and those other idiots. Did you know they think I'm a lesbian?"

"They probably don't," Alex says. "They're just being bitches."

"Alex," I say, putting my finger on his chest. "Don't say 'bitches.' It's rude."

"OK, OK, sorry," he says, backing off a little. But I don't give up. I get closer to him.

"Do you think I'm a lesbian?" I ask.

"No," he says, looking me in the eye.

"Do you think I'm pretty?" I ask. I can't believe it, but the words just come out.

"Of course," he stammers. "You're prettier than those dumb other girls." I barely let him get the words out before I put my arms around his neck and kiss him. His lips taste like salt. Probably fries. It's so brief that it hardly registers beyond that as Alex pulls away almost immediately.

"Hey," he says, unwrapping my arms from around his neck, "we'll get in trouble."

"I don't care," I say. "Señora Chang won't suspect anything."

"No, it's not that, it's …"

"What — Jane?"

"You know I think you're awesome, Rosie, but maybe let's just be friends for a while, OK?"

"OK," I say. *I don't understand. Wasn't he giving me all the signs that he liked me on the field trip?* "Don't you like me?"

"Of course I like you."

"I mean … do you like Jane?"

"Yeah, I mean, she's my friend. You're both my friends."

"Oh." *There's my answer.* "OK."

"Hey," he says. "It's OK. We can just pretend nothing happened."

But Alex's attempt to smooth things over doesn't help in the slightest. I get out of the darkroom as quickly as I can and slam the door behind me. I see Señora Chang look over, and I can tell she's noticed we've both been in there for a while. I look around, and everyone is staring.

"Sorry, I have to go home. I think I'm sick, I have the flu or something," I mutter quietly, and run out of the door and walk home, skipping the wait for the bus.

I'm in no mood for Dad's nonsense when I get home. I slam the front door to let him know. But he doesn't understand social cues too well.

"Rosie, I wanted to talk to you," he says.

"Dad, I'm really tired. Can we just eat something and talk another time?"

"Honey, I feel like you're not being very nice to Alison."

I can't believe him. I'm clearly upset, and he wants to talk about his stupid girlfriend.

"Well, what about me, Dad? You just brought her around all of a sudden."

"I'm sorry, honey, but you haven't been that easy to talk to lately."

"That's not fair."

"Well, I'd like us to try again. Let's all have dinner together again."

"Sure, fine."

I see the expectation in his eyes.

"Tonight?" I ask.

"Yes, perfect! We can go out and get pizza. I'll pick her up now. "

He goes to grab his keys. I can feel the tears welling up again.

"I'm not hungry," I reply and then go to my room.

The truth is, pizza sounds amazing. But I'm not about to go chow down with that bimbo right now. I spend an hour doing seven pre-algebra problems and eventually hear Dad leave the apartment.

I close the book and walk around my room. Karen sits on my desk, staring at me almost expectantly. I pull out my sketch pad, walk to the phone and dial the number written inside. It rings a few times and then goes to the answering machine.

"Hi, it's the Hendersons," I hear her mom's voice say. *It's so bi-*

zarre to hear her voice after all this time! "Please leave a message at the tone. Thanks for calling!"

"Hi. This is message is for Karen. It's Rose ... it's Aubrey. Aubrey O'Connell, from Galena. Um ... it's so cool that I saw you again. I can't wait to talk to you more. I hope you're feeling OK these days, and ... um, just call me back. Bye!" I say, leaving our phone number.

I sigh. It would've been nice to talk to her after all this time. It's probably too late. I'll try again another day.

I go back to my room and read a little bit of "To Kill a Mockingbird" before switching off my lamp, but my mind is too busy to fall asleep. When I close my eyes, the scene with Alex plays out in my mind. I shake my head, but then Emily's stupid face and her dumb pigtails bounce around in my brain instead.

The next thing I know, I hear the sound of something slamming against my closet door. I wake up, unsure of what time it is. My eyes adjust to the dark, and I look over to where Karen was sitting on my desk. I don't see her anymore.

I sit up and look around. Karen is across the room, lying by the closet door as if she had been thrown. Like I did the other day. *But how?*

I look toward my bedroom door I see the Shadow Man standing there.

The room is cold. He turns his featureless head toward me. *No! No more Shadow Man. It's under my control.* I close my eyes and try my trick. *Maybe if I just close my eyes for long enough, he'll go away. I'll fall asleep again and this will all go away.*

But it's no use. When I open my eyes, he hasn't moved.

"I don't know ... who you are," I say finally, as sternly as I can. "But leave me alone."

"I can't," he replies in his soft, gentle whisper. "I'm a part of you now."

My mind scans back to the day of the field trip. The details are fuzzy, but I remember that the cars were standing still in the middle of the road. That's how I knew.

"It was just a dream," I say. "This is just a dream."

"Are you sure of that?" he asks.

I'm not so sure. *It was a dream. I woke up and everything was normal again. But ... it felt real. I could feel him like ... like he was underneath my skin, living inside of me.*

"At my birthday ... was that you?"

"You called out to me, didn't you? Didn't I give you what you wanted? A scare for you and your friends?"

"That's not what I wanted," I say.

"You don't even know what you want," he says, inching toward me along the left side of my bed. "You don't know who you are. You don't know anything, do you?"

"Who am I, then?" I reply. I don't know why I say it. It just comes out.

"Who are you? Are you Aubrey Rose? That sad girl from Illinois who none of the boys like because she's too shy? That mousey girl none of the girls like because she's too weird? Is that who you are?"

My breath quickens as he moves closer to me. His face gets close to mine, and I can smell something. It smells like ... smoke.

"That's ... not me," I say.

"No, that's not you," he says, his head moving away from me. "You're Rosie. What you want to happen *will* happen."

His voice seems to come from all around me, his words floating in the air.

"What do you mean?" I ask.

"You should hit her in the face next time," he says.

CHAPTER 32

I wake up and stumble out of bed. I try to remember everything that happened during the night. But I can't think clearly.

I remember the shadowy figure in my room, but I can't recall him leaving. I just remember the feeling that ran through me while he was there, like my blood was running cold. I wish I could remember what he said to me. I wish I could make him go away. But I can't. Or maybe part of me doesn't want to. As if he gives me the power to do what I would never do on my own.

I shuffle into the hallway and see Dad brushing his teeth in the restroom. I try to get him to let me stay home, but he's having none of it. "You're fine, Rosie," he says coldly. "Let's get you to school."

My head bobs multiple times in first period. Ms. Sailor notices, but she doesn't say anything this time. My last two essays were basically gibberish, and I never did go speak with Ms. Torres like she asked me to. By this point she's probably given up hope for me.

I trudge down the hall toward second period, where sometimes I bump into Jane going in the opposite direction. *I wonder if Alex said anything about what happened yesterday. God, I hope not.*

I see her walking through the hall in her Gap sweater, hunched forward with her arms crossed.

"Hey," I say, waving cheerily.

"Fuck off," she says without even looking at me as she brushes past. I hear one of the eighth grade boys go "Ohhhh" from behind me. I tell him to shut it and then notice Nora standing still near me.

"Did you like watching that, Nora?" I turn and say to her. "Do you like watching me get embarrassed? Well, congratulations, now I'm just as miserable as you are." I start to walk away.

"I'm sorry, Rosie."

I freeze and turn around. "Sorry for what?"

She doesn't say anything.

"Did you put a curse on me?" I ask.

"What?" she says, laughing a little.

"Did you put a curse on me to make Alex hate me?"

"What are you talking about?"

"Whatever, Nora," I say, bumping into her as I walk the other way. Nora drops something, and I turn and look to see a folded piece of paper on the ground. Nora turns, red-faced, and runs down the hall. I bend down and pick up the piece of paper and see that it's a note addressed to me, folded up. I stuff it in my pocket.

In science class, I read the note. In it, Nora tells me all about how she appreciates that I tried to reach out to her when no one else would. She was scared because the last time someone did that, it turned out to be a mean joke. Her home life hasn't been so good, and her only friend moved away. It's like I'm reading a note from myself. I feel so terrible after what I said to her that I want to cry. But another part of me takes over. *She deserved it*, I think.

I try my hardest not to fall asleep as the class drags on, but I can barely keep my head up. Mr. Minogle walks around, moving his hands wildly as he talks. I can't hear anything he's saying, though. My eyes go blurry. I watch his shadow move up and down on the wall. *If I squint, it looks just like ... him.*

When the bell rings, I collect my giant backpack as quickly as I can. When I drop a pen, I just leave it there. I sense someone trying to speak to me when I walk out into the hall, but I don't turn around.

"Hey Rosie, maybe you should try Starbucks."

It's Emily. I hear Lauren's stupid jackal laugh behind her. *I can't take it anymore. I can't.* The Shadow Man's empty face flashes into my mind. I feel his vacant eyes behind my eyes.

I turn around and punch Emily right in the face. She falls back on Lauren, her blonde pigtails bouncing around her bloody nose.

"What are you doing?" Lauren screams. Emily holds her face and doesn't say anything. Mr. Minogle walks out of the door and grabs me by the arm, dragging me to Mrs. Sailor's office. I don't know what happens to Emily; I imagine she's headed for the nurse's office. All I know is that I've completely lost control of myself.

CHAPTER 33

Mrs. Sailor is pissed. She's jotting something down on a notepad while I sit across from her. Her usual mile-wide joker grin is nowhere to be seen. I don't dare budge or say anything. But I don't really feel anything either.

"Rosie," she starts. "Can you tell me just what the in world happened?"

"I …" But I don't know what to say.

"I just don't understand it. You're a great student. You have some of the best grades in our whole seventh grade class. Ms. Torres thinks the world of you. But lately she's been a little bit worried, and frankly so am I."

I stare down at a scratch on her desk. I wonder how it got there. *Maybe it was some girl like me being yelled at by someone like Mrs. Sailor who doesn't understand anything. Maybe she was just trying to get free.*

I realize that Mrs. Sailor is talking again. "Emily isn't talking. She won't even say who hit her, and neither will Lauren. Mr. Minogle thinks it was you, but he didn't see it happen. No one else was there."

Mrs. Sailor pauses expectantly. I can feel her staring at me. I want to look up and confess everything. But I just stare at the scratch on her desk, and I don't say anything.

"Rosie," she says quietly. "Is there something you want to tell me?"

"I …" I say again. I look up at her. But I don't see her. I see *him*. I see those eyes. Staring so vacantly. That emptiness pours into me, looking right through me.

Then I answer Mrs. Sailor's question. "I don't know. Emily's a popular girl. She's so nice and smart, too. I don't know who would want to do something like that to her."

Mrs. Sailor's eyes narrow. *Now she's really pissed.* But I don't meet her gaze. It has no effect on me.

"Ms. O'Connell, don't you get smart with me. You're treading on very thin ice here. Now, is there anything happening at home that you want to talk about?"

What, you mean ghosts telling me what to do, leading me places, sometimes hurting me? "No."

"I know you haven't had an easy transition …"

I stop listening.

"… your mother's death earlier this year …."

Mrs. Sailor's words scramble like alphabet soup in my brain.

"Did you know that Emily's father died last year?"

I sit up in my chair. "No. I didn't know that."

"She hasn't had the easiest time, either. I had hoped … maybe you two would become friends because you both had such awful experiences. But that doesn't appear to be the case."

I can't believe it. But … there's no excuse for the way she treated me. She still got what she deserved. Mrs. Sailor is talking again.

"… with that said, Rosie, can you tell me what happened?"

"… I said I don't know."

"You … don't know? Well, frankly, I don't know either. I don't know what would happen to make one straight-A student hit another one in the face, but since neither of you is talking, I guess we won't find out any time soon. You'll both be suspended for the rest of the day …"

I stop paying attention to whatever schoolmarm nonsense Mrs. Sailor dishes out now that she's done playing psychologist with me. I could tell her about what I'm going through. About how Emily and Lauren have been tormenting me all year, how they even damaged my belongings and drove me to tears multiple times. But what good will that do? That won't excuse my behavior. I'm pretty sure I broke Emily's nose. And I'll be labeled a tattletale at school.

I could try to explain about how Dad doesn't pay attention to anything I do and treats me like a nuisance. But that won't matter either.

And I *could* try to tell her about the shadow people. How they say things to me. And take me to strange places that are familiar and yet totally alien at the same time. But that part — that's the part that would matter. That's the part that would get me sent away somewhere terrible. And maybe they'd be able to figure out what was wrong with me. Maybe it would be better. But most likely, it wouldn't. I'd lose the few friends I have, although I'm pretty sure Jane hates me now that I tried to kiss Alex. And there's no telling if the shadow people would stop coming, anyway.

So I don't say anything. Mrs. Sailor tells me how disappointed she is and sends me home for the rest of the day. Dad is pissed but I think it's more because I've interrupted his writing session. He's colder than usual to me on the way home. "Honestly, Rosie. This time … I didn't think you actually would …" is about all he can muster. I still don't say anything. He sends me off to Vera's for a while, and I'm glad to be out of our apartment.

Luckily, Dad hasn't filled Vera in about what happened, and Vera doesn't pry into why I'm home so early, other than asking, "Are you sick, dear?" but I shake my head. Dad says that he needs to take care of some things and would she mind watching me for a bit. Vera never really does seem to mind, and I think Dad knows that. I think Vera gets lonely when it's just her and Jimmy.

I watch TV blankly while I wait for Jimmy to get home. "Jerry Springer" is on. I feel like one of those people now — like an animal, violent because I can't stand up for myself properly.

It's all over for me at school now. Emily will probably get one of her minions to kick my ass, probably Mia or one of the other volleyball girls. Yearbook is probably done — I don't think Señora Chang will tolerate my behavior and won't talk to me about music anymore. I'm pretty sure Alex is grossed out by me and Jane hates me for trying to kiss him. I don't even know why I did it. I guess I wanted him — anyone — to notice me. And Dad cares more about his work than he does about me. I'm just an inconvenience to him. These thoughts trickle through my brain, but I can't feel anything about any of them. It's like I'm staring at the thoughts, which are like little raindrops, barely registering before disintegrating.

Jimmy finally gets home. "Rosie!" he says, excitedly. He's excited to see me. It's sweet. Jimmy's gotten a lot taller since I first met him. He's about as tall as me now. His voice has changed, and he's grown into his ears. Girls at school would probably all have crushes on him if he wasn't ... different.

"Why are you here?" he asks. Jimmy isn't one for tact.

"Jimmy, that's not very nice," Vera says, with understanding behind her eyes. "Rosie's always welcome here."

"What're you watching?" he asks.

"Nothing good," I say.

"I'll be back in a bit, guys," Vera says. "I'm gonna do a few errands and bring back some food."

"You don't have to get me food," I say. "I'm sure my dad ..."

"It's OK, lovey. Really."

She leaves and is gone for a couple of hours. It's by far the longest amount of time Jimmy and I have been alone. I flip off the TV.

"Hey!" Jimmy cries.

Jimmy doesn't like it when I turn off the TV once he's been watching a while, but I feel like I'm going to burst.

"Jimmy, I need to talk to you," I say. I try not to startle him, but I know I sound frantic. "Remember ... remember how you told me that day that you had seen something in the apartment? But I didn't listen to you? I'm really sorry about that."

"Seen something?"

"In the apartment. When I was talking to those girls at school?"

"Oh yeah," Jimmy says, a little disinterested.

"Jimmy, listen. What was it that you saw?"

"I ... can't remember."

"Was it a man? A dark man?"

"A dark man," he repeats back to me. "I saw someone outside."

"Where did you see him?"

"He was coming out of the apartment at the end of the floor."

Has Jimmy been seeing them this whole time? "Jimmy, this is important. What did he look like?"

"He was tall. It was very dark. He came to the window."

"Did he talk to you? What did he say, Jimmy?"

"He held up a cat."

"... What?"

"He held up a cat and walked away."

"Oh. Jimmy ... that was just Mrs. Lieberman. She wanders around sometimes at night."

"You said it was a man."

"No," I say, disappointed. "It was just her and ... Coco, or Peanut."

"Did you get kicked out of school?" he asks suddenly, without looking at me.

"What? Where'd you hear that? No, just for today. I guess I did."

"Did you really hit a girl in the face?"

"Um," I say. I don't know what to say. "I'm sorry, Jimmy."

"Why are you sorry?"

"I don't want you to be scared."

"I'm not scared. I'm not a little kid!"

"I know that. Sorry."

"Stop saying sorry!"

"OK," I say. "It's just that ..." The thoughts won't even form into sentences. I just start to cry and Jimmy, to my surprise, comes over and hugs me. And it's not quick like last time — he holds me for longer, knowing how bad I feel. I haven't been held like this in ... I don't know how long. Since Mom. I cry into his shoulder. And then, before I know what's happening, I kiss him.

Only then does Jimmy pull away suddenly. He stares at me. At that moment, the door opens and Vera walks in with armfuls of grocery bags.

"Hi guys," she says. "Sorry it took so long. I'll whip you up something fast."

Jimmy cries and then runs out of the room. I hear him whimpering in the other room, and Vera goes to tend to him. I don't know what to do, so I sit holding my legs. When Vera walks back out, her face looks stricken.

"Rosie," she says. "What did you do?"

"I'm sorry," I say, tears streaming down my cheeks. "It was an accident."

"Did you get suspended today for hitting a girl?"

I don't say anything.

"Jimmy doesn't lie," she says. "Honey. I'm sorry, but I think it's best if you went home now."

This upsets me almost more than anything else that's happened. She calls me "honey" like Dad does. Not "lovey" or "Rosie Posie" or any one of her other fun nicknames. Just "honey." I hate that.

I grab my giant backpack and trudge back to my apartment. Dad isn't home, as usual. This time, I'm glad about it. I don't want to see him or anybody. All I want to do is sleep and forget this day ever happened.

I curl up with my pillow clenched between my legs and arms and try to cry out the pain of today. But I feel empty. I try to think back to the things that I did. *Did I really yell at Nora for no reason? Did I really rat out Marty because I thought he might be the Shadow Man? Did I really try to kiss both Alex and Jimmy? Did I really lie to Mrs. Sailor? Did I really punch Emily in the face?* I feel like those things happened, but I was watching someone else do them. Like I was floating somewhere, doing these things and watching myself at the same time. It was like the dreams ... but this was real life, and I know that I did these things because I wanted to.

I toss and turn. It's cold, but I'm too lazy to get under the blanket. Luckily, Mom is there to tuck me in and put a blanket over me. She kisses me on the forehead. I roll over to say good night to her. But Mom isn't here. She hasn't been here. *Dad?*

I sit up in bed. The Shadow Man is standing there again. He's more fully formed now. Tall and dark, with a faintly glowing outline. His head pulsates like a heart beating on the outside, and there's no face to speak of. The smell of rot and smoke permeates my nose. We stare at each other in silence.

"Rosie," he says finally. "You did well."

I rub my eyes. *It's just a dream*, I tell myself. Maybe if I do my trick, he'll go away. I close my eyes, then open them. He's stepped closer to the bed, so that he's now right at the foot of it. I gasp, and it feels like all the air has been sucked out of the room.

"What do you want from me?" I cry.

"What do I want?" he says, cocking his head to one side. "What do *you* want?"

I don't answer. I don't know what I want or what he even means.

"Do you want to keep living this life? This life of misery?"

I can't answer him. I don't know the answer.

"You aren't loved here. Your school, your friends, your family. They're all gone."

"What the hell are you talking about?" I say finally. "They're all here. You're not here. You're not real!"

I feel my body lying itself down without me telling it to. My hands go down by my sides and I feel rumbling coming from beneath my bed. Could this just be a dream? The rumbling gets worse, heavier, louder. *It must be an earthquake. We're having a*

California earthquake, and I'm asleep, this is a dream.

I can't move, but my eyes look straight ahead. The Shadow Man is still there, unflinching as pieces of the ceiling fall down. The walls start to crumble, and my bookshelf tumbles down, landing right next to the bed. Finally, the floor collapses beneath the bed and I'm falling, sinking farther and farther into nothingness. I can see night sky above me. I float up into it, sudden and fast, flat on my back with my arms outstretched. I feel like I'm falling upwards at a million miles an hour.

"Dad!" I cry out as I'm shooting upwards in bed.

"Honey, what is it?" Dad says, running into the room.

I look around. It's morning. The bookshelf, the ceiling, everything is where it was before. My pillow is drenched in sweat, but there's no other sign of anything out of the ordinary having happened.

"Was there an earthquake?" I ask him.

"I don't know, honey. Did you feel one?"

"I think so."

"Well, then we probably had one! Your first California earthquake." His cheery demeanor doesn't help. "Come on, honey. I let you sleep in a bit. Let's get you ready for school."

"Dad," I say. "I think I'm still suspended."

"Oh?" he says. "I thought it was just for the day."

"No. Today, too." I'm lying, but he can't tell.

"OK then, Rosie. You just get some rest."

I wait for him to give me a kiss on the forehead or pull the blanket back over me, but he doesn't.

CHAPTER 34

I've never lied to Dad before in my life. Not about anything serious, but I can't face school again. Maybe not ever.

Dad's gone somewhere by the time I get up. I look around the kitchen for a note, but, of course, he hasn't left one. The answering machine blinks. I usually don't bother checking it since it's mostly Alison leaving messages for Dad, but I think it might be him calling me to let me know where he is. I press play to hear my voice saying "Hi, this is the O'Connells?"

"God, I need to re-record that. Everything I say sounds like a question. I hate my stupid voice—"

I'm cut off by the message left by a familiar girl's voice.

"Hi Rosie! It's Karen. I seriously can't believe we ran into each other like that. It's, like, fate, or something. Listen, um, I'm not sure if I can come see you again. I'm sorry. I hope you understand."

I sit there dumbfounded. *Why wouldn't she be able to see me after all this time? Am I that uncool?*

"... It's just that ... well, anyway. I hope you're doing good. I'm doing really well, I really like my school and California is awesome, I hope you think so too. I'm not sick or anything ... I'm not sure why said you hoped I was feeling OK. Maybe I had the flu or something the last time you saw me? Anyway, yeah, things are good, and ... you just take care, OK, Rosie? Miss you—"

"End of message," a woman's prerecorded voice says.

What the hell? Why did she act like she had no idea what I meant? She sounded and looked so normal. Is it possible she was cured?

I pick up the phone to call her again. The dial tone buzzes into my ear, but I sit staring at the wall. *I guess she just doesn't want to see me again. Maybe it's been too long.* I hang up.

I must seem really crazy. Or I must be really crazy. Karen must be a totally different person now. Like Jessica was. Why would she want to be friends with me?

I walk around the apartment in a daze. *I need to find out what's happening with me. Or things will never get better.*

I get ready to leave the apartment. I'm not sure where I'm going yet, but I know I'm not going to find the answers watching TV alone.

It's an unusually cold, gray day, so I don my fake military jacket from Target over my T-shirt and sweatpants and start the day as I would have during the summer, walking down the halls of the second floor and running my fingers along the railings. *I saw something here before ... the shadow of the railings ... turned into someone. I remember now! Then I walked over here ... no, it was the other way. The Shadow Girl wanted me to follow her. She wanted to show me something.*

The Shadow Girl ... where has she been? Did I send her away forever? Did the Shadow Man kill her? I mean, wasn't she already dead ... or something?

I can see her now, clear as day in my mind. I follow the railing to the staircase and walk down, past Mr. Ennis' closed door.

Here, at the bottom of the stairs, the Shadow Girl walked underneath, and I followed, into ... the other place. *Is this where they're coming from?* I reach into the darkness and grab onto a hand.

"Ahh!" I scream.

"Oh! What you doing down here, mama?" Mr. N says.

"I thought ... I'm just home sick from school, and I thought I saw something weird down here."

"Down here?" he says in confusion.

"Yeah," I say. "I know it's dumb. What's in there?"

"You want to see what's in here?" he asks.

"Yes," I reply.

Mr. N turns around and unlocks the door. He turns the knob and pulls it open. It's pitch black, and it occurs to me that I might be in danger. This is definitely a bad idea. Mr. N's hand reaches upward. Before I can register what's happening, he's yanked his hand down, pulling the chain to a lightbulb, revealing a small room with a water heater and some large-headed brooms.

"You hear a weird noise here?" he asks. "Probably the water heater. It's old. Need to replace soon."

I stare into the room, looking for an answer. I remember the neighbors gathered here for some unknown reason. I remember the staircase. The awful hands.

"OK, mama, let's go," Mr. N says.

He walks me out to the courtyard where Elena stands dressed in a green caftan, her silver sequined slippers peeking out underneath.

"Mama is sick," Mr. N says. "Take her for some tea?"

"OK, mama, I'll take care of you," Elena says, draping her arm around me and ushering me into their apartment.

The Negrescus' apartment is a parade of iridescent shades: patterned drapes and painted walls, jade eggs and lamps dangling with jewels. It's a glittering emerald city within what would, from the outside, seem like just any old apartment.

"I love your home," I say.

"Thank you, dear," she says. She puts on some jasmine tea, and we sit at a circular glass table adorned with a green felt and polyester tablecloth.

"How you feeling?" she asks. For a second I relish her thick accent and warm demeanor.

"Oh, I'm not sick. I'm just ... I'm not sleeping good. And I got in trouble at school."

"Ah, poor mama. Drink some tea. You feel better."

I sip the hot liquid, and it's a little bitter, but it does make me feel better.

"Now, Rosie," Elena says. "What's really wrong?"

"I don't know," I say. "You guys are really nice to me and my dad. But ... I think there might be something wrong with this place. Or there might be something wrong with me."

"Something wrong?" she asks. "Tell me."

I hesitate, but the softness of her eyes and the warmth of the tea makes me feel comfortable. *What's the harm in telling her? Maybe she'll understand.*

"I see things," I say. "In the night. I can't tell if they're dreams or not."

"What kind of things?"

"Sh-shadowy figures," I say. "There's one who looks like a girl. She seems to want to help me. Then there's one that's like a mischievous little boy. Or a dog, or both. And then there's one ..."

"Who?"

"A tall man. He's not like the others. He tells me things ... things that I don't want to hear."

I don't know what possesses me to tell Mrs. N all of this. I wasn't intending to go this far into it, but she listens intently.

"Mmm," she says finally. "Mama, what does your father say?"

"Huh? Oh, I haven't told him about any of this. He wouldn't get it. I mean, I don't understand myself what's happening to me."

"Ah. Yes." She stands up. "More tea?"

"No, I'm good."

"Well, it sounds like mama has a lot on her mind. I miss being a young lady. Such imagination! You make a great storyteller someday."

"I'm ... I don't think I'm imagining it," I say. I see a hint of recognition in her eyes, and I jump on it. I follow Elena into the kitchen, where she's pouring herself more hot water. "I saw you."

"Who did you see — me?"

"Yes, Mrs. N. I saw you. In the room beneath the stairs."

"Oh, I don't go there. That's Mr. N's work."

"No, it was different. In the middle of the night. You were there. Everyone from the building was there. Mr. N, too."

"Mmm," she says. "And what were we doing?"

"You were just watching me. I followed the Shadow Girl ... up some stairs. And I could hardly move. Everyone ... seemed to me pushing me along. They wanted me to see something."

"What did you see?" Mrs. N asks. I realize she's clasping my hand.

"I don't know ..." I think about Mr. Ennis, sitting in his chair, smoke swirling into the air, and I press further. "Who is Mr. Ennis?"

"Who is he? Why, he's our neighbor."

"But who is he? Where did he come from? And why does he have that sign on his door?"

Elena walks slowly back to the table. I follow her and sit.

"Some people," she starts. "Some people … have very hard lives. Mr. Ennis — you see him walking with a cane, yes?"

I nod.

"He had polio, as a boy. He lived near here, with his mother. She had to fight to pay for his bills all her life. But they could not pay. Their house was taken, and she never spoke again. They came to live here before anyone else. Later, she died … of sadness. And he could barely walk after that. He had to crawl around like a little doggy. It's so terrible," she says, waving a hand.

"I can't imagine Mr. Ennis saying all those things to you," I say. "He seems so quiet."

"Well, he didn't say them with his voice."

"What? What do you mean?"

Mrs. N points her red acrylic nail to her head. "He told me here."

I look deep into her glassy eyes. "The shadow people …"

"They want to help you," she says. "Everyone. You …" She clasps my hand again. "You are in great danger, mama."

"Everyone," I say, thinking about the blank faces of everyone in that room.

"Only here," she says, holding my hand to her chest. "They don't know it here," she says, holding her hand to her head.

"What do they want to show me?"

"They cannot show you what you will not see," she says. "You must see it on your own."

"Who is the man?" I ask. "The Shadow Man."

She sits back. "He is … pure evil."

"Why does he want to hurt me?"

"He cannot," she says. "Not yet."

"What can I do?" I say, jumping to my feet. My eyes have teared up.

"You must open your eyes," she says, fanning out her red nails in a spiral.

CHAPTER 35

Before I can ask any more questions, Mr. N arrives back home. He tells me Dad is looking for me and asks that I return home. At the door, he whispers, "Take care of yourself, mama."

The door closes behind me and I'm left bewildered. *Did I just imagine that conversation? How did she know about the shadow people?*

The Shadow Boy. He led me to the dirt pit. What was there?

I head out of the apartment complex and over to the construction site, my head still swimming from my conversation with Mrs. N. It looks like some work has been done on it: more lumber has been put up and the frames are starting to resemble real stores. I walk around the place before descending into the dirt pit.

It was here ... in the center. The rain came. I couldn't get up the walls fast enough ...

My thoughts are interrupted by loud barking. At the top of the pit, I see two pitbulls standing above me. They growl menacingly, and the sound cuts right through me. *The outline of their ears ... the wolf in the road. The outline of her hair as we approached. It looked like we'd hit her.* I stand frozen, the thoughts racing through my mind until the snarling dogs jump into the pit and launch their attack against me. I run as fast as I can and scale the side of the pit. The dogs follow close by, barking and nipping at me. *The wolf in the road. A warning. Did she try to warn me then?*

I call out from deep within. "Help me!" I scream as I try to pull myself up and out. The dogs are getting inches away from me, jumping and trying to make their way up the steep side of the pit. I struggle toward the top, and one of them lunges, grabbing a mouthful of my jacket. As it yanks me backwards, I see a man's hand shoot down toward me.

I grab onto the hand, but the dog still has my jacket in its teeth, its jaws tightly locked. I start to fall backward.

"Rosie!" a familiar man's voice says. "Let it go!"

I shake the tattered military jacket off of me, then find myself pulled upwards by Alfonso. He puts his big arm around me, and we run as fast as we can away from the construction site. We stop to catch our breath once we realize the dogs have stopped their chase. I cry into Alfonso's gray workshirt.

As we stand there, the long, black town car drives up to us. The man in the sunglasses rolls down his window. I hear barking from the backseat. When he takes off his sunglasses, I see the Shadow Man's blank eyes stare at me. I shut my eyes and cower into Alfonso's shirt again, trying to quiet his menacing voice that whispers unintelligibly in my mind.

"She was trespassing," he tells us coldly. I look up, and the man's eyes have returned to normal.

"You could've killed her!" Alfonso shouts, his voice shaking. He points at the man. "You're sick. What is the matter with you? She's just a girl."

"You're fired! Get out of here, you Mexican trash," the man says.

"C'mon, Rosie," Alfonso says. He leads me back to the apartment. We walk in silence, his arm around me.

At the front gate, I stop. I'm so sorry," I say. "It's my fault that I got stuck in there. You got fired, and it's all my fault!"

"It's OK, princesa," he says. "It's OK. Don't worry about it. It's not your fault."

 "Where's your dad?"

"He's home," I say.

"Oh. You go home to him, OK?"

As I walk inside, I can't look back at him. I'm so embarrassed and horrified at how he was treated, and his only concern was my safety.

"Rosie," he says. "Take care of yourself, will you?"

I finally turn around, but Alfonso is gone. Back inside, I'm alone again.

CHAPTER 36

I walk upstairs slowly. The Shadow Man lingers in my mind. Elena. The wolf. The pitbulls. The man in the town car. He was in Dad's script. I can't make sense of any of it.

I come to a halt as I reach Mr. Ennis' apartment. The door is open, and he's standing at the screen door in his bathrobe with his cane, as usual.

He never walked after that. He crawled around like a little doggy. Elena's words echo in my mind. I turn and face Mr. N through the screen door. He stares unflinching, his wispy, white hair gathered like feathers around his brown, wrinkled head. He's not wearing his dark shades this time. I look directly into his shimmering blue eyes. The saddest eyes. The eyes of the Shadow Boy.

"Mr. Ennis," I say. He glances downward. I'm ashamed of how I looked at him—how I looked at all of them, everyone who lives here—like they were monsters out to get me. I put my hand against the screen door. I can't say why. He lines his hand up with mine, for just a second, through the screen.

"ROSIE!" Dad screams from the top of the stairs. Mr. Ennis drops his hand and walks away from the doorway, into the darkness of his apartment. I hurry to the top and meet Dad, who takes me by the arm and scoots me back inside.

"What are you doing wandering around like that?" Dad asks. "You had me worried."

"Worried?" I ask. "Since when are you worried?"

"I do worry. Rosie, I'm doing everything I can to give us a better life. Alison's father … Don't roll your eyes at me!" Dad says, grabbing me by the arm again.

"Ah, Dad, stop!"

"You listen to me, Rosie. Alison's father is a big-time Hollywood producer. And your father just sold his first screenplay! Can you believe it? They're gonna make my movie!"

"Dad," I say. "That's great."

"We won't have to live in this horrible apartment building much longer. Just be good and wait. Can't you just be good for me, honey?"

"Be good," I repeat, as though I don't understand.

"Yes," he says. "What is with you, anyway? You walk around like a zombie, day and night. And now you're getting into fights at school? That isn't the girl I know. That's not my Rosie."

"Do you even want to know?" I ask. "Do you even care?"

"What are you talking about?"

"Do you know what's happening to me? Do you see them too? Or do you just ignore it?"

"Ignore what? Rosie, you're not making any sense."

"I'm sorry I don't make sense, Dad. And really, I'm so happy for you. I'm sorry I'm not the daughter you thought I was. Did you know that I had my first kiss, Dad? Did you think to ask me how things were going for me?"

"Honey," he says. "You might be too young for that."

"It went horribly, Dad, since you asked. And I kissed Jimmy, too, the autistic neighbor boy. Wanna know why?"

Dad stays silent, staring at the couch.

"Because … I don't have anyone else, Dad. Mom's dead. She's dead, and you could barely contain yourself, you were so ready to move on from her, and from me, to your new life in L.A. And now I have no one."

"Honey, that's not true. You'll be with me forever."

You'll be with me forever.

"I don't need you," I say. "I have the neighbors. Vera, Mr. and Mrs. N, even Mr. Ennis. They're here to protect me."

"Protect you? From who?"

"From them. The shadow people."

"What in the world?"

"The people who come at night, when you're asleep or off having sex with Alison …"

I don't feel the slap. I just feel the weight of my body hit the ground and I stay there while everything spins above.

CHAPTER 37

"You ..." he begins. "Just when things are finally going right in my life. Just when things are *finally* happening. Rosie, do you know how hard it is to land a deal in L.A.? It's not a fairy tale ..."

But I can't really see him anymore. In my mind, I'm side by side with Karen again, on the swings. We stare at each other in perfect bliss, swinging higher and higher. She jumps, as she always does in the dream. But this time, I see her land. She's fine. I follow her and jump. It's too high. I land and twist my ankle.

But we're not alone. I'm sitting and holding my ankle, crying, and Dad walks over and sees me. I reach out to him with one arm, but instead he goes to Karen. He picks her up by the arm and shakes her. I can't hear what he yells at her. All I feel is pain. And I remember her family moving. Her father shouting at mine and them nearly coming to blows. Then the police came. I overheard Mom say they dropped the charges, and they moved away. And I never saw Karen again.

And I remember the knife. Cutting my finger on it. Mom came over to scold me. And Dad slapped her so hard she fell against the wall. "Why would you let her play with a knife, you stupid bitch?" The words echoed through my skull and fell out the other side.

I remember playing hide and go seek with Mom in the house after Karen moved away. Running up and down the stairs until Dad screamed at her so much that she stopped playing with me altogether.

And I remember walking down the hallway to the closed door of their bedroom. I could hear noises, thumping sounds. I clutched my stuffed dinosaur and walked closer. Then the door opened. I saw Dad, his eyes alight. Mom was in the corner, slumped over and crying. Bedsheets and papers were everywhere. "Rosie! Go back to bed!" The words echo around in my brain, and I hold my head and close my eyes.

But he never turned on me. Until recently. Thoughts of these moments flood my brain. *Shaking the bed to wake me up in the middle of the night every time he had a new idea for his script. Screaming after me I tried to cook us macaroni and cheese and burned my hand on the stove, leaving me to deal with blistered hand alone. Me finally telling Dad about the girls and boys at school and Dad telling me to "pop them one in the mouth ... that oughta shut them up." Me sneaking out in the middle of the night to get away from him. Coming home. Him tightening his grip around my chest and shoulders, stopping himself before he got to my neck. Him going back into his bedroom, leaving me bruised and dazed, stroking Karen's hair.*

"Rosie. Rosie! Get up."

Dad clutches me to his body like a baby as I sit up. "I'm so sorry I did that honey. You have no idea how close I am to changing everything for us."

"For you," I whisper.

*

I awaken from a nap to find Dad has taken the time to make pasta. I haven't had anything except pizza, sandwiches and frozen dinners in so long, save for Vera's cooking. It's such a nice surprise that I almost forget everything that happened earlier.

"Rosie!" Dad says, turning around while he stirs sauce. He has that wild look in his eyes again, but he holds out his hand.

"I want us to start over. This can be a new beginning for us, everything that's happening. We'll get out of here and finally be happy. Here." He ladles sauce over the spaghetti. I sit down at the counter, famished. I chow down and instantly start to feel better.

Dad cleans up as I'm finishing.

"Dad, aren't you gonna have any?" I ask.

"Honey," he says. "I wish things were different … If only you could have supported me more. If only you could have appreciated everything I've done for us."

"What are you saying, Dad? I appreciate …"

Dad's irises have gone white. His head starts to bulge outward and become oblong, His skin greys and becomes ethereal until his entire being is dark, grotesque. I see *him*, standing in the kitchen where Dad was, faceless, his white eyes boring holes through me.

I drop my spoon and push against at the counter, sending my plate flying across the kitchen where it bounces and spills bright red sauce on the tile floor. I taste something bitter on the back of my tongue and don't recognize it as my own bile until I'm on my knees, doubled over. The Shadow Man slowly approaches from behind the counter. His cold arms wrap around me and lift me up. I feel myself being carried to bed.

"Dad," I say. But the featureless face does not look down. It carries me to my room and lays me on the bed.

CHAPTER 38

I can't move. I feel my hand being manipulated. Something is being placed into my hand. It's small and cylindrical, but I can't look. The Shadow Man stands in front of my bed facing me. With a sudden, inhuman leap, he's standing on the edge of my bed, looking down at me.

"This is what you wanted, isn't it, Rosie?" it asks in a disembodied voice.

"No ..." I mouth, but no sound comes out. "Rosie," I mouth to myself, looking out the window of Dad's car.

"Mom," I mouth. "Mom," I say out loud. "Mom!" a voice cries out from deep within me as my whole body convulses. My eyes glance ahead, and the Shadow Man is gone; I see the Shadow Girl standing in front of me.

"Rosie," she says. "You did it."

"I did?" I whisper.

"You saw me. You helped me remember. You sent him away."

"Mom?" I whisper.

"Yes, dear. It's me."

"Mom ..." I say. "I ..."

"You must get up."

"I can't."

"You must get up and leave this place. Now," she says, placing her hands on my feet. I see her fingers spread around me. The shadows envelop me, covering me with warmth. With that, she looks at me one last time. I see her face — Mom's face — before it fades away. I cry out and sit up. The Shadow Girl is gone.

I feel a rumble and hear the sound of the water heater groaning. The sound rises into a roar, an awful tearing sound, and the rumbling grows more powerful. I leap out of bed. My legs float an inch above the ground. I kick my legs, trying to move, but I'm suspended in the air while the floor begins to buckle beneath me.

"Go," says a whisper behind me, and my toe catches the ground.

I run from my bedroom and out into the main room. To my surprise, I see Jane there, standing in the middle of the room with her backpack on.

"Jane!" I cry out in a weak voice. "We have to get out of here!"

But she can't hear me. She walks right around me and into my bedroom.

"Jane!" I cry, turning around. Jane's not there. Where my room used to be is a swirling vacuum. My bed, my desk, the walls, all crumble into the center, tumbling like laundry in a washing machine.

I'm on the verge of floating away, pulled by the space where my room once was. I reach down to grab on onto the carpet. My legs rise farther into the air as the hole sucks everything into it. I look backward to see that my legs aren't legs anymore. They're black streaks of shadow. Pieces of me break off like crumbs and float into the swirling mass.

Rosie, pull away, Mom's voice echoes into my mind. *Pull away or you'll be lost.*

I grab tufts of carpet and scale along the ground, slowly making my way out the front door.

The apartment complex is illuminated in bright fluorescent light that casts shadows onto each door. My legs float like tattered clothing above the rumbling ground. I scrabble along the walls and propel myself through the corridor. Finally, my legs begin to take shape and become human again. I pedal them until I regain my footing and run down the stairs.

The rumbling seems to have subsided, and the courtyard is empty and cool in the night. I stop and look around. *Could this be over?*

My eyes turn to the stairwell to see the Shadow Man standing at the top. His head cocks, as if he's egging me on. I'm not about to wait to find out what he'll do to me. I run to the back door of the complex and find it tight shut. I press on it with all of my body, but I feel weightless, and it won't budge. Behind me, I see the Shadow Man floating down the stairs toward me. His arms are outstretched, palms out, and he moves slowly and steadily through the night air.

"The stairs," I hear her voice whisper. I run from the back door and toward the stairwell that leads to the parking garage.

I pass the mailboxes, then look through the garage gate. There's nothing unusual: parked cars surrounded by small pools of oil and water. I find the button to open the gate, but my hands won't seem to work. I look down and see that my fingers are curling and tightening.

I hurl the backs of my hands against the garage door button. It's painful and it takes a few attempts, but the door finally opens. I take a step into the garage and my foot immediately sinks slowly into one of the black pools of sludge. I turn back to see the Shadow Man standing at the top of the stairwell to the garage.

I can't delay a single second. I reach down, but my hands are still rigid. I stare at my hand and focus, mentally prying my fingers apart. Finally, they relent enough so that I can grab my own leg and yank it out of the muck. I tumble but pull myself up and run across the garage. The sound of twisting metal pierces my ears, and I look around to see the cars bending like paper and sinking into the sludge. More sludge has appeared around my feet, and I'm sinking again. The Shadow Man stands on the other side of the garage, watching me sink with his empty eyes.

I pull with all my might and take one slow step at a time. Each step is more difficult than the last. Whipping my head around, I see him. This time he walks with alien precision, each foot landing neatly and gingerly as he approaches me.

The gate groans as it begins to close. I close my eyes and feel warmth around me, like hands pulling me up. I'm floating again. A picture enters my mind: it's Mom, holding me in Lake Michigan in the summertime, teaching me how to swim. I start pedaling my feet, sending me slowly through the air. My feet catch the ground. *There's no time to get stuck again.* I lift my feet one in front of the other, until I'm almost at the gate. The gears and chains whir unsympathetically. *This is my last chance!* My soles stick, and I pull my feet out of my sneakers and slip through the gate just as it closes. I run forward a few steps, then turn back. He's at the gate, holding onto the bars like a prisoner. His oblong head morphs into a thinner shape, and he sticks his head through the bars. His neck stretches, and his head moves toward me with liquid motion.

"Keep going," a whisper says. I move away and run along the sidewalk, barefoot.

The air feels off as I run along the sidewalk. No cars hum along the street. It's a dead space. The streetlamps hang overhead, their harsh fluorescent light glaring. It feels worse than before, hot and blinding. I look up and the lights shatter one by one, sending down shards of glass. I run toward the construction site, guided by something I can't explain, much less understand.

It's so dark now that I miss the curb before the site. I trip and go tumbling into the ditch, mud smearing across my clothes and hair. I roll into the middle of the pit and lie there breathing heavily. The mud bubbles and gurgles around me.

Was it him guiding me to my demise this whole time? Is he using her voice?

My head lifts and I see him. Not the Shadow Man, but the Shadow Boy, standing on all fours, crouching near me. His blue eyes look at me with quizzical compassion.

"Help," I say, but the words barely come out. I look at him and try connect with him wordlessly. But it's hopeless. He's sinking into the ground just like I am. And the Shadow Man is standing at the top of the pit, glaring down at us.

The Shadow Man ambles downward, his movements precise and twitchy, gliding effortlessly across the mud like an insect across a lake. The boy sits and stares up at him. The Shadow Man places a hand on the boy's head and pushes him further down into the muck until he's nearly submerged.

The Shadow Man stands over me. I try to raise my head, but it falls back down. Mud curls around my arms and hair like fingers. I feel roots in the ground writhing around me. Mrs. N's outstretched fingers fan out in my mind.

"Dad," I say.

The Shadow Man looks down at me.

"It's you, isn't it?"

He doesn't speak.

"You're here to kill me. Like you killed Mom."

Hands appear all around me, propelling me forward.

"Rosie," the Shadow Man says finally. It's Dad's voice, only distorted, muffled. "Did you always know?"

I lie there in silence for a moment. "Yes. I chose not to see."

The shadow hands have disappeared, and the writhing roots grapple around my feet. I feel my legs beginning to sink into the muck.

"Why?" I ask.

"Now nothing will stand in my way."

"Dad," I ask. "Did you ever love me?"

He stares down at me. He doesn't answer.

I can see Mom's smiling face in my mind. "Mom," I whisper. "Mom!" I let out a scream from deep within. I see her, the Shadow Girl, floating overhead. Her hair trembles in the wind, and her arms stretch out in a star shape. My mind races. *The hands. Mr. N's cigar smoke as he stares out the door. Or is that Mr. Ennis? Who is he? He is the boy. The boy who is doomed. What did the sign say? I ran past it so many times.*

"The hands that pull to the earth," I say out loud.

The Shadow Boy's hands appear out of the dirt beneath the Shadow Man, my father. They grasp around his legs and become part of them, two long, globular masses of black. The Shadow Man's head tilts down as he starts to sink slowly. He reaches his arms up as he sinks beneath the mud.

I stand up.

"Rosie!" my father's voice calls out.

"I know that you never loved me," I say.

The Shadow Man's hands stretch upward as he sinks further down. The pit becomes a sinkhole, sucking down the mud and everything around it. I stare for a moment, before realizing the danger I'm in. I start climbing up the sides, jamming my hands into the muck, but it's no use. It's coming down in chunks, a muddy avalanche that I can't navigate. My hair is plastered in cold, wet mud that sticks against my face. But I see something. Fingers reaching down. A hand. Or something in the shape of a hand. I grasp onto it. I feel warmth. It's glowing. Now my hand is glowing, too. The iridescent light creeps along my skin, slowly illuminating my entire body.

I start to float upward. Up, out of the sinkhole, away from the ground. At first, I'm like a balloon that's been released. But it's as if I suck in more helium with each breath and start to fall upward, faster. I look up. I see her, star-shaped above me. The Shadow Girl. I remember a photo of Mom on the mantelpiece, holding her father's hand as a child, a Christmas tree with the brightest star shining in the background. Every time my parents fought, I would stare at that star and imagine being inside of its light. I would invisible, the words around me becoming a foreign language.

I float toward her glowing shape, and the light envelops me. It's blinding. I can't see anything now except that warm, white light, wrapping around me like a blanket. Everything is gone now.

CHAPTER 39

I pull the blanket up to my chin, but I don't open my eyes yet.

"Aubrey!" a familiar voice calls out. Could it be her? My eyes open. It's my Aunt Rita.

"Oh Rosie, thank God," she says. She leans over me, kissing my forehead. I'm still in a daze.

"Are you ... really here?" I ask her.

She laughs. "Yes, Rosie," she says, wiping away a tear. "I'm here now." She grasps my hand and gives me the kind of look she used to give me when she knew I understood something that the other kids didn't. It's as if we communicate telepathically.

"Dad is ... gone, isn't he?" I ask.

"Yes," she says. "They—they don't know where he's gone, but he's missing."

Aunt Rita regains her composure. I try to focus on features. Her curly, dark hair seems to spring up and down from her head. Her eyes and sharp nose swim around her face like goldfish. I close my eyes to stop the movement from making me nauseous.

"Just stay right there, Aub," she says, running to grab the doctor. A middle-aged Indian woman in a white coat walks in with a clipboard. She instructs me to lay back down until my vision stops swimming. After a few customary questions, Aunt Rita asks if we can be alone, and she obliges.

"I know you just woke up, but ... it's very important that you tell me what you remember," Aunt Rita asks.

My memory streams back to the awful time with The Shadow Man. The Shadow Boy's sacrifice. Finally seeing my mother and hearing her voice.

"I just remember eating spaghetti," I say.

Aunt Rita laughs. "That's good. What else?"

"Something ... something was put into my hand. A bottle."

"They found a bottle of your mom's medicine in your bed. It looked like you had taken it, so the doctors pumped your stomach."

"I didn't take it," I say. "He did it. He put it into my food."

"Who did?"

"The sh ... Dad."

"Dan," she says, under her breath. "How could you ...?" Aunt Rita's voice starts shaking and she turns away from me.

"Aunt Rita?" I ask. "I have to know. What ... really happened to Mom?"

Aunt Rita lets out a pained yelp. She covers her mouth and faces the window before turning to face me after a few moments. "It's why they thought you took them ..."

"What? What are you saying, Aunt Rita?"

She walks over to the hospital bed and sits next to me, once again placing her hands on mine. "They thought you were too young to understand. Your father did, anyway. That's what he said."

"Understand what?"

"Your mother ... was getting better. I'm sure you knew that."

"I did. I thought she was, anyway."

Aunt Rita takes a deep breath and shuts her eyes. "They thought your mother killed herself by taking a lot of her medication at once. That's what it looked like. That's what the toxicology report confirmed. And because of that ... well, they thought you did the same. But I knew, honey. I always knew that wasn't right. I knew your mom wouldn't have left you like that. Not ever. She wanted to live ... for you. And I knew you wouldn't have done that either."

I stare forward for a moment letting what she tells me wash over me. She continues.

"You and your dad left so abruptly that it confused everyone. He didn't leave a forwarding address or phone number or anything. Did you know that your friend Jessica coming to visit was the first anyone had heard of you both for months? She gave me your number, and I called. I called so many times and left messages. I guess he didn't play those for you, did he?"

I don't say anything.

"He answered the phone once. It was silent, but I knew it was him. He sat there, breathing heavily, like some sort of animal ..."

"Aunt Rita?"

"I'm so sorry, Aub. I shouldn't be upsetting you with all of this information right now. The important thing is that you're safe."

"I knew."

"What?"

"I knew. About all of it. But I chose not to see."

"Oh, Aubrey ..."

"I'm Rosie now," I say. In my mind, Dad and my conversations leading up to the move play back in fast forward — how he started calling me "Rosie" leading up to the move, suggested using it as a first name. How did I not see through that? "It was his idea to change it."

"He must have wanted to throw off anyone who was looking for you," she says. "You don't have to keep it, Aub."

"I want to keep it," I say. "I'm different now than I was before."

"OK, then. Rosie it is."

"How did they find me?"

"When you didn't show up for school the next day, your friend Jane got worried and went to the office. They gave her some catchup work to bring you, but when she got there, she found the door open and food spilled on the kitchen floor. She saw the empty bottle in your bed and ran to grab your landlord."

"Mr. N?"

"Yes, that's it. And your super ..."

"Alfonso."

"He said he saw you wandering around the building in a daze. Your elderly neighbor, Mrs. Lieberman, I guess she saw you through her window, ambling toward the construction site next door. They went and found you lying in the mud ..." Aunt Rita's voice cracks, but she pulls herself together. "You were lying there with your arms stretched out toward the sky."

"They did all that? Oh my gosh. How did they get ahold of you?"

"Your neighbor, Jimmy. He told his aunt to call me, and they found my number in the phone book."

"Jimmy ... I didn't think he was listening when I told him about you."

"Aub ... Rosie, if they hadn't been there, you wouldn't have made it. You've been unconscious for two days. But you're going to be OK. You're OK!"

"Aunt Rita?"

"Yes?"

"I'm sorry. About Mom."

"You don't have to be sorry," Aunt Rita says, hugging me. "You don't have to be sorry about anything."

*

I tell the doctors and the police everything I remember about what happened before I passed out. I tell them what I know about Mom, too. How he treated her when we were growing up, and how he started to treat me. He started to cook for her when she got too sick. That's when he probably did it, I told them. Her medication was very strong. Too much of it could've killed an adult, much less a 13-year-old. The police suspect that Dad murdered Mom so that he could cash in her life insurance policy and move to L.A. to fulfill his dream finally. I guess that's when I became too problematic for him.

I don't tell them about anything else. The things I saw and felt. I know they were real. But no one else would understand.

The police keep searching for Dad. They question Alison, her father, the neighbors, his strange acquaintances from the "industry" and all of us in the family. But they don't find any signs of Dad. His keys and wallet are still in his room. There aren't even any footprints, or any other sign that he fled. He's just gone.

When I'm released, I stay in a hotel for a bit with Aunt Rita. Mr. N comes to visit and tell me he changed all the locks in the building, and he gives me a new key to the apartment.

Finally, I'm allowed to return home to the apartment building with Aunt Rita. I wonder why she stays with me for so long. I later learn from her that what's happened with me has coincided with her divorce. So, it's convenient, in some sick way.

Vera and Jimmy hang out with us every night, and I start going back to school. Everyone — Vera, Jane, Alex, Jimmy, Ms. Torres, Mr. Minogle, Mrs. Sailor, even Emily and Lauren — is overly apologetic and treats me kindly. People at school find out what happened, and I'm something of a celebrity for a while. Even though I'm still sort of out of it, things get a lot better in terms of people being nicer to me.

At the same time all this happened to me, Mr. Ennis died in his sleep. It was about a week before anyone knew. Alfonso had to burst the door down when he didn't pay rent and realized something might be wrong. I kind of think Mr. N knew already, though. At least Mrs. N probably did. After cleaning out Mr. Ennis' apartment, Mr. N took down the sign on his front door. No more despair for Mr. Ennis; he was finally at peace.

Aunt Rita moves in with me and after a while decides we should be in a proper house to give us a fresh start. I agree, although I know I'll miss the place. I promise to stay in touch with Jimmy and Vera and have them over from time to time. I get to stay in my same school, which I've grown to like, and Alex, Jane and even Nora Nagy are my best friends.

Leaving the apartment for the last time, I give Vera and Jimmy the biggest hugs. I chat with everyone — the mother and her twins, Alfonso, Mrs. Lieberman.

I run my fingers along Mr. Ennis' door as we're leaving. Someone new will be moving in the day after we leave.

Mr. and Mrs. N give me the biggest hugs of all. I turn back to them before I leave.

"Mr. and Mrs. N?" I say. "Thank you."

They nod in understanding. I walk outside and wonder if I'll ever see them, or the shadow people, ever again.

*

Wonder what happens when Rosie goes to high school? Sign up for our mailing list to get the latest news about the Shadow Series and get free "lost chapters" from "Rosie & the Shadow People."

Acknowledgments

Thank you to all of you who helped make this book happen: my wonderful husband for listening to me talk about this nonsense for two years, my parents for their constant support, Zoe Aarsen for your help and mentorship, my illustrator Kim Herbst, my editors Max and Tim Major, and all of my readers and sounding boards: Tiffany, Kate, Nick, Christine and, as always, Velma.

About the Author

A.M. Sandoval is an author, musician, and freelance writer and editor born, raised and living in Los Angeles. He has one dog and dreams of having many more. "Rosie & the Shadow People" is his first novel.

Made in the USA
San Bernardino, CA
10 December 2019